All the rich people had disappeared.

Guppy woke up one morning, huddled in rags on a cold street – and they had all gone. So had their cars, their possessions, and their money. All that was left was the broken city, with its crumbling buildings, stagnant canals and pitted roads: and the broken people – the unwanted, useless ones, cast away and forgotten: the *Abandonati*.

Guppy looked around him. 'Place is a mess,' he told himself, as if noticing it for the first time. 'Whole place is a goddamn mess.'

He inspected the boots he had found three days ago, pulled himself upright and started to walk down the middle of the road. He was going to find out where the rich people had gone to, for there had to be something better than this . . .

Garry Kilworth's funny and moving fable charts the odyssey of down-and-out Guppy and his companions on the road to find the rich people and a better life. It is a forceful and haunting reminder of a need for social responsibility and humanity in a world that is swiftly losing both.

ABANDONATI

ABANDONATI

Garry Kilworth

UNWIN
PAPERBACKS

LONDON SYDNEY WELLINGTON

First published in Great Britain by the Trade Division of
Unwin Hyman Limited 1988

First published in Great Britain by Unwin® Paperbacks, an imprint of
Unwin Hyman Limited, in 1989

UNWIN HYMAN LIMITED
15–17 Broadwick Street
London W1V 1FP

Allen & Unwin Australia Pty Ltd
8 Napier Street, North Sydney, NSW 2060, Australia

Allen & Unwin New Zealand Pty Ltd with the Port Nicholson Press
Compusales Building, 75 Ghuznee Street, Wellington, New Zealand

British Library Cataloguing in Publication Data

Kilworth, Garry, *1941–*
Abandonati.
I. Title
823'.914 [F]

ISBN 0-04-440391-7

Set in Palatino
Printed in Great Britain by
Cox & Wyman Ltd, Reading

To Maggie Noach,
the other half of the team

The word *abandonati*, like *graffiti*,
is rapidly becoming international.
The street people, homeless or
mentally ill, with no place to go,
no square inch of the earth to call
their own – these are the *abandonati*
– the abandoned ones, the unwanted,
castaways from our society.

Not with a bang,
but a whimper.
T. S. Eliot.

Chapter One

Hey sizzle-diddle
The cat's on the griddle –
Little dog's better,
If you can get 'er.

A feral cat glided out of an alley and into the sunlight. It stopped, looked about it cautiously for a few moments, then navigated a hill of rubble. A pile of rags beside the broken bricks and plaster suddenly came to life. A hand flashed out and grabbed the cat by its tail. The cat screeched, whirled and used its claws and teeth, sinking them into the hand, which released its grip instantly. Then the creature streaked away, down another alley, and out of sight.

Guppy sat up abruptly and sucked at the wound the cat had inflicted. He cursed the cat, and himself, with a parched throat, knowing that he should have caught the animal by the neck. Breakfast would have to wait now.

Dawn was always late in the streets. It had trouble driving away the cold shadows: the more lethargic ones that lay heavy in the alleys and under the overhangs of rubble. Guppy looked about him, blinking rapidly. He scratched his grizzled chin, realising that he had not had a decent drink in three days: not since that can of cleaner he had found under the stairs of some building.

He ran his fingers through his matted, greasy hair, wondering what to do. His head was muzzy and his thoughts frayed and worn. Drink. He needed booze of some kind.

He could see a group of people huddled around a fire at the bottom of the street and decided to ask them if they had any spare water. It was coming to something when he had to drink water, but they sure as hell weren't going to give him liquor.

1

He stumbled to his feet, hitching up his baggy trousers, the crotch of which hung almost to his knees. He needed a piss. He relieved himself against the wall. Then he carefully folded his ragged blanket, his only possession, and tied it with a piece of string around his waist. Then he staggered towards the circle around the fire.

Like himself, they were dressed in rags and most of them clutched some form of blanket. They watched him coming towards them with blank eyes. One of them, a young boy, threw some fuel on the fire: an old book or something. Guppy approached them slowly, warily, and then stood there while he considered what to say. The words were difficult to form.

Finally, he blurted out, 'Got any drink? Anythin'? This terrible thirst, see.'

No one replied. There were some open mouths, but little comprehension showed in the eyes. Only the boy seemed to grasp at his meaning.

'Park's over there,' said the kid. 'Over behind.'

'Thanks,' said Guppy. There was usually some kind of water in a park: a pond or canal. Last time he had drunk such water it had made him sick for two days, but he could get some and boil it first, on their fire, if they let him.

He staggered to the corner, then remembered that he hadn't got anything to carry the water in. He went into the first doorway he saw, stepping over the rubbish that had collected in the opening. Inside it was damp and smelled of cats and rotting plaster. There were people lying in the hall and in the side rooms. It took even longer for the dawn to reach indoors. Someone had been sick at the end of the hall and it reeked, offending even Guppy's insensitive nostrils.

He found what used to be the kitchen, when the place had functioned as an apartment. There was a pile of empty cans in one corner. He took one.

On an impulse he tried one of the taps, twisting it back and forth. It was hard to turn and squeaked. No water came out and Guppy moved away from this useless device to the more reliable source in the park outside.

It was a canal and though full of trash, it looked a bit cleaner than most. Guppy was so thirsty he decided to risk it. They might chase him away from the fire anyway, and it took a while to boil the water and let it cool. He wanted a drink *now*.

He gulped down the cold water, filling his belly, which immediately churned, noisily. Then he took something which looked like putty out of his pocket and though it was grey with dirt, crammed it into his mouth and swallowed it quickly. It tasted good. He stared around him then, wondering whether or not to go back to sleep.

Suddenly, as he stared through the trees and down the long streets, a dim but interesting thought came into his mind. He stared at the murky water running through the reeds. He looked up and around him, at the tall buildings, some of them still having unbroken windows here and there. He glanced with distaste at the scabby cats and lean dogs that roamed well out of his reach.

'Place is a mess,' he told himself, as if noticing it for the first time. 'Whole place is a goddamn mess.'

He inspected his footwear: boots wrapped around with rags. They were a good pair. He'd found them only three days ago. Too big, but that was better than too small. He might get a few blisters as they slopped around, but that was all right. Blisters were nothing when you had sores up your legs that wept continually.

He pulled himself up, to a near military posture, and then, setting his eyes on the middle distance, began to walk. He went out of the jungle of the small park and into the potholed street. He started off, down the middle of the road, intending to stop for nothing. *He was going to walk out of the city.*

As he began his journey his aches slipped away from him, and his head began to clear a little. He found less need to cough. His penis still stung, after that piss, but he still felt pretty good. He felt okay. This was an adventure. He was going to walk out of the city. He was going to walk and walk, day and night, until he came to . . . to . . . to something – something that wasn't the city any more. He knew that the city was big, but it couldn't go on forever. There had to be something – an edge – another side – something more than just crumbling buildings and pitted streets, with grass tufts growing like hair from the cracks in the concrete.

As he trudged through the dilapidated brick world, he passed many groups of people, some standing around street fires, others sitting on the steps of buildings which were their homes. Guppy knew there wasn't much inside these places, but at least they provided some sort of shelter from the coldness of the night. These groups tended to live in pockets. Most of the areas were uninhabited.

Guppy had some vague idea that it might be spring, and that hotter weather would be coming soon, but he'd been wrong about that before. The trouble was, if he could find something to drink, he would, and it almost always made him forget things. That's one of the reasons why he drank it. Once, he had found a whole bottle of pure, amber whisky and he had to hide in a cellar before opening it. Otherwise people would have smelled it and come from all directions.

He passed the remains of a dead baby, lying in the gutter. There was not much left of it, but he noticed the tiny bones. The dogs had been at it. Guppy was not fond of dogs. They could get pretty nasty if you tried to take something away from them. Anyway, it was best to let them eat. They would get fat on the meat and with a rod and snare you could catch one of them. Dogs made a delicious meal. It was one vicious circle. When had it been any different?

'Everything's broken,' he said to himself.

It seemed that it was all coming to a head. There was so little food around and soon . . . soon . . . he didn't know what to think next. People would die, he supposed. But they were already dying or dead. Lots of them.

There had to be a place somewhere, where people were better off. It hadn't always been like this. He could remember when the streets had cars in them and people were dressed in good clothes and carried packages bought at shops. Now all that was gone. He didn't know where it had gone, but wherever it was, lots of the people had gone with it. He was just one of those that had been left behind, abandoned because he was useless.

Oh yes, there had been a better time than this. Of course, there had been street people then. Guppy had been one of them. He had been brought to the city as a boy of six from a place they called . . . called . . . he couldn't remember, but it

4

was a bad place anyhow. That's why his aunt had come to the city. But at the time about two-thirds of the population were already on the streets and all that happened was that Guppy and his aunt joined them.

Still, there had been markets that sold vegetables, and you could get cabbage stalks that had been thrown into the gutter at the end of the day. You could make a soup with that. And you could stop rich people and ask them for money. You could even join a gang and steal things. You could live quite well.

But gradually, there came to be more people on the streets than in the houses. And those who had houses were no better off, in the end, because there was no work to do and they had to sell all their things. The time came when nobody wanted those any more. All they wanted was food. Money was no good. You couldn't buy anything with it.

Then all the rich people must have left. Guppy didn't know where they had gone, but the street people, the *abandonati*, talked about this betrayal all the time. They were bitter about it, savage in their condemnation, as they huddled around plasterwood fires, spitting into the flames. No one seemed to know precisely when the abandonment took place, but they were all sure it happened. The ones in the know had up and left, taking their possessions with them, and had spared not a thought for those that remained behind.

Guppy didn't know where they had gone. He had been drinking hard around that period, and nothing seemed to make sense anyway. He just knew that he woke up one morning and realised that all the wealthy people were missing. He'd sort of noticed that the cars were becoming fewer, but he didn't exactly remember when they had *all* gone. Seemed like it happened just one morning.

Broken glass crunched under his feet as he walked. The sun glinted on old cans and glanced off shattered shops, the broken panes like huge, jagged-toothed mouths. It was no use looking inside. There was never anything in them these days.

At one place he saw someone with a wooden box, the front of which had a grey glass screen and some buttons with numbers on them. The woman with the box smashed the glass, kicked the innards – a mass of wires and bits of plastic – out from inside. Then she threw the box onto a fire. It burned brightly but

5

with a stink. It was made of plastic, obviously. Guppy stopped to watch it melt into globules spurting colourful flames and noxious gases. He could see the woman was disappointed.

That night, Guppy killed a rat by kicking it against a wall when it ran past him. He was good at that. He joined some people and cooked it over their fire, giving away the front legs. One of the men asked him where he was going.

'Walk,' said Guppy.

'Where though?'

'Out of the city. Gonna walk 'til I can't walk no more, that's what. Must be something there.'

The people around the fire nodded thoughtfully.

'Why don't you all come?' said Guppy.

There were some looks exchanged then shakes of the heads. He could see he had frightened them. They didn't want to go out, into the unknown. At least where they were was familiar to them. They knew places to forage. They knew where to find water. These things were important and could not be given up lightly.

'Trouble with you is,' said one of the women, 'you don't belong to no street tribe. This tribe here, see – us – ', she pointed to the people around the fire, 'we look after each other. You – you're just a oncer, on your own, with nobody else. We got responsibilities. We got to protect our places and when the kids grow, we got to tell them where to find water an' how to cook nettles an' grass roots.' She paused. 'See, if we move off, someone else – another street tribe – they'll move in. We'll lose our watering places and have to fight to get 'em back. Up here,' she tapped her head, 'is where it's all kept these days. You got to know where to look for things, 'cause if you forget, you die of thirst or worse. I got little stories I make up to tell my kids where the watering places is – to help 'em remember.'

'Like what?' asked Guppy, interested. This was the first time he had heard the word 'tribe' applied to groups of people, but then he didn't go near many groups and when he did they often wouldn't talk to him.

'Like I might say to them, there was once a giant, bigger'n the tallest building, who slipped an' cracked his head just where the redbrick meets the yellow. This giant's brains spilled down a drain nearto, and into the water underneath the street.

There they growed into mushrooms, each little bitty part of brain. That's where you'll find water and mushrooms, there, under the place where the redbrick meets the yellow . . . then I go out and show them where, an' they know an' remember, so's to pass it on to their kids, see.'

Guppy nodded thoughtfully. He was trying to recall where he had seen redbrick buildings converging with yellowbrick, so that he could go tomorrow and get some mushrooms for his churning gut. But probably she had made that up.

'Okay,' said Guppy, 'but I'm going to find out what's going on. Where the people have all gone to. I bet they're living in big houses on the edge of the city, with lots of food and whisky and stuff. I bet.'

'What people?' asked the woman, whose eyes seemed to be burning inside her skull. Guppy noticed that her gums were swollen and bleeding and she had spots of dried skin on her face.

'Why, all those people that were here before.'

'Before what?'

Guppy started to get angry. She was making him think about things he had no answer to. There was a sort of bleak, black cloud in his head when he thought too hard about such things.

'I don't know before what,' he grumbled. 'I just know I saw people, driving around in swanky cars and wearing fancy clothes . . .' he did not mention that he still saw them sometimes, ' . . . and now they're gone. They just disappeared and they must have gone somewhere. You tell me before what.'

The woman snorted, hunching closer to the fire.

'They got poor like us.'

'No, they didn't, they couldn't have done,' shouted Guppy, 'because there's not enough.'

'Not enough what?' asked a man.

'People. There should be more around. They just up and left somewhere. I'm going to find them.'

He kicked at the fire in protest at this *tribe*, who had forgotten that they had all been abandoned. Some sparks flew and there were some growls from one or two of the tough-looking men. Although he was not afraid of them, Guppy decided to behave himself.

The next morning he was up early and walking. One of the women had told him he would soon come to a district where the buildings were taller and reached right up into the clouds. She was right. Guppy found it a pretty scary place, because the woman said the buildings were haunted by the spirits of gods or something. Whether she was right or wrong, it didn't matter. They were scary enough: just the sheer height of them. They seemed to lean over you as you walked and Guppy was afraid one of them was going to fall on top of him and crush him to catmeat.

Guppy kept on walking. It was only later that he realised that the woman might have been scaring him away from the place because there were tribal secrets connected with it.

'Place is probably crawling with mushrooms,' he muttered to himself, angrily.

He spent another night under a stone bench, by a bronze statue. The statue was of a man on a horse. The man was holding up a piece of paper, only it wasn't paper, it was green metal like the rest of him. There was a triumphant expression on the man's face, as if he had just found himself a bottle of booze.

The next day, Guppy walked some more, but he got tired and hungry. It started to rain and he used his hat to catch some of the water, but it didn't help his hunger at all. He found a park where some trees were just coming into bud and he ate the buds. They tasted rather sweet. Then he found some wild onions amongst the grasses and ate them too. They tasted sour.

He started walking again.

That evening he found another street tribe who had killed a dog and they gave him some. He slept by a woman who put her hand under his blanket to feel his penis, but when it didn't get hard she left him alone. Guppy felt sorry that he could not respond, because the woman had a kind face, but she already had a child who was sickly. He got warm with her though, which was pleasant. In the morning she gave him a fish thing that had some oil on it. It was the best food he'd tasted in a long time and he wondered whether to stay with her, but then remembered he had something to do.

He started walking again.

Three days after that, he came to a halt. He stared bleakly in front of him. The streets stretched endlessly away, towards a horizon hidden by tall buildings. He looked behind him and to both sides. There was nothing but crumbling brickwork melting into cracked concrete. He was never going to get out. The place was a prison of shattered blocks of stone. Even the clouds above looked as though they were made of something solid, like dirty alabaster; the sky some kind of stained crockery.

As he stood and ruminated on some biltong he had stolen from a window-sill, wondering whether to join one of these new street tribes with their defined areas to support them, a machine came round the corner. It tried to cling to the kerb, but kept swinging out of control, crashing against walls and already bent lamp posts. It was going too fast, for a robot street cleaner. Low and flat, like a small river raft, it careered dangerously close to him, as it sucked away with ineffectual vacuum snouts at the surface of the road. He kicked a foot at it, missing.

Then there were rapid footsteps and a figure came flying around the corner, chasing the street cleaner. It was a thin little man, his ragged coat many sizes too large for him, flapping like a cloak in his wake. His weasel-like face was pinched with breathlessness as his protruding eyes fixed themselves on the disappearing machine.

'Out of the way. Out of the way,' he yelled at Guppy, who was standing right up on some steps by this time.

'I ain't in it,' shouted Guppy indignantly, as the man ran past him.

'Well, make sure you ain't there the next time,' cried the other over his shoulder.

Guppy shook his head in wonder.

'Goin' like fart in a draught,' he said to himself. 'Where's he going in such a hurry? There ain't no place to go to, that ain't like where he's been.'

Guppy, alone once more, looked around for somewhere to spend the night. There were few people in this part of the city. He decided on a doorway with a porch, and began gathering some window-frame wood to make a fire. Then he remembered he hadn't got anything to start the flame with, so he abandoned that idea. He was sitting on top of the steps when the little man reappeared, walking slowly back down the street.

9

Chapter Two

Little Tommy Tucker
Sings for his supper –
Tommy hugs his mother's head –
Sing on, Tommy, mummy's dead.

'Catch her?' Guppy asked the skinny guy, as the other came up alongside the steps.

The man paused to stare at Guppy. His coat now touched the ground, the hem scuffed and worn with loose threads trailing after it. The buttons on it were huge, though two of them were missing. Beneath this magnificent garment the little man wore a bright yellow waistcoat – at least, it had been bright at one time, as one or two patches attested, but now it was mostly just yellow. A scrawny shirtless throat came out of this waistcoat: the neck of a turtle. The sleeves of the overcoat were rolled into large quoits, from which claw-like hands protruded. He used one of these extremities to pick at his nose.

'Naw. Goin' too fast. I'll get him one day.'

There seemed to be some sort of confusion as to the gender of the street cleaner, but Guppy didn't feel like arguing about it. He was more interested in why the thin man wanted to race about after useless solar-powered machines.

'What do you want her for?'

'I want to get up there.' A hand pointed dramatically towards the sky.

'To the top of the buildings? What for?'

'Naw, you dope. The sky – out into space. That's where those bastards have gone. They all went out into space, lookin' for a new world. Left us here – the bastards.'

Guppy nodded. 'I thought they'd gone somewhere.'

'Well, that's where they've gone. I got this plan to build this space ship and follow them. They don't get rid of me so easy. I'm a good mechanic. I can take parts of things and do wonders with them. You wait and see.'

'Maybe I won't be around to see it.'

'Why – where you going?'

Guppy thought about this, pondering on the problem for a long time, while the other waited patiently at the foot of the steps. There was plenty of time for such decisions.

Finally he said, 'No place, I guess.'

'In that case, you can help me build my space ship. I need another guy to help. Only got one pal, and he don't believe that's where they've gone, so he don't get too enthusiastic when I talk about it.'

'What's your name?' asked Guppy.

'Rupert. An' my pal's name's Trader.'

'I'm Guppy,' said Guppy. 'This Trader – is he a nice guy?'

'Oh, yeah. We been together a long time. You want to join us? We got some food. Trader's got a hidey-hole full of cans. We eat like kings.'

'You sure don't look like it,' replied Guppy, observing the leanness of the little man.

'Aw – that's just nervous energy. I'm a big man in a small body, see. Got to keep moving all the time. Get the twitches if I sit still too long. You sure you believe me – about the people being in space?'

'I knew they went somewhere,' confirmed Guppy.

Rupert smiled, broadly. He looked very happy at this reply, though Guppy was still a little suspicious as to why anyone would want to share food with him.

Rupert said, 'You come an' meet Trader. He won't tell us where the food's stashed, but he keeps it coming all right. We had peaches yesterday.'

Guppy couldn't remember what a peach was, but it sounded good. Then something came up from the smoky regions of his memory. Wasn't a peach something to do with a woman? They called women peaches. He backed up the steps a little.

'You ain't cannibals, are you?' he said. 'I got nothing against it, you understand, it's just I can't hold it down. I keep thinking of the meat walking along the road and talkin' like you and me – then up it comes.'

Rupert screwed up his face in an expression of disgust.

11

'Hell, I ain't *never* eaten people. You catch diseases like that. You never know what they died of. Naw, this is all canned stuff and to my mind they never put people in cans. Sometimes it may look like it, but it's usually squid or somethin'.' He paused. 'You coming?'

It wasn't that Guppy did not want to go with this man who had shrunk inside his clothes, but now that cannibalism had surfaced in his brain, he was worried that he was being led into a trap. Maybe these two guys wanted to eat him? That sounded more likely than the idea that they would give him food for nothing.

'You got any booze?' he asked. 'Any good liquor?'

'You kidding? Who the hell's got good booze these days? Even Trader ain't got that.'

Guppy's fears dissipated. If this man *really* wanted to lure him into a trap, then he would have promised him the earth.

'No harm in asking, is there?' He joined the other in the road. Rupert smiled, slapped him on the back, and then led him down a side alley. They walked for about a quarter of a mile until they came to a house jammed between two tall skyscrapers. The door was half open and hung on a single hinge only. Guppy followed the coat inside to a room off the hallway. It was furnished surprisingly well, with an old armchair, a table and some rat-eaten rugs on the floor. There were some straight-backed chairs too, and a cabinet, with the glass missing, in one corner.

A large black man, with white, wiry hair and beard, was sitting in one of the straight-backs. He got up as they came in and looked hard at Rupert.

'Who's this?' he asked.

Guppy quailed. Surely he *had* been led into a trap? This bulky man looked as though he ate seven or eight people a day.

'This is Rupert,' said Rupert, winking at Guppy. 'I ain't been gone that long.'

The humour was lost on the bigger man.

'No – him. The guy with you.'

A thick dark finger was pointed at Guppy, who had the urge to run from it before it exploded or something. Trader looked very annoyed. His jowl quivered as he talked. When men the size of Trader got annoyed, you either looked for a handy piece of four-by-two or got the hell out.

'He's a friend. Gonna help me get my space ship together. You leave him be, Trader.'

'Whose food is he eating?' demanded the other.

'He can share mine. You don't need to worry yourself about your precious gut. He can have half of mine.'

'Look,' said Guppy. 'I don't want to start no arguments. I just . . .'

Trader turned on him.

'You got any sugar?'

Guppy trembled.

'No – honest.' He paused and then said, 'Sugar?'

'You need sugar to make wine.' Trader moved across the room, mumbling, 'If I had some sugar, I could make us some wine. Plenty of bramble berries in the season – got some canned fruit in any case. If I had some sugar and some yeast, I could make wine. Damn rats have been into everything that wasn't surrounded by metal. All the sugar's gone. See,' he turned to face Guppy once more, 'you mash up the fruit and put lots of sugar in. The sugar turns to alcohol and the yeast helps it ferment. Actually, you can do without the yeast if the fruit's a little rotten, but you can't do without the sugar. It just makes mouldy fruit juice otherwise.'

Guppy's mind fixed on sweet things. He wanted to impress this big man and get on his good side.

'We could get some honey. What about that? There's still bees in the parks. We could get some honey.'

Trader shook his head.

'Nooo,' he said, with beautifully rounded vowels. He had a very cultured voice, which made Guppy feel ill at ease. He distrusted intelligent people and an accent like that usually denoted an educated user. 'Nooo, that won't do at all, will it?' The last two words were completely opposite in tone from the rest of his reply, which had been full of confident rejection of the idea. They were a plea.

Rupert said, 'Could be that honey might do it, Trader. Maybe you got yourself a partner too, in this Guppy? Maybe he's been sent to help us both?'

Trader came right up close to Guppy, who could smell his breath. It smelled of beans and it made Guppy feel hungry. However, Trader seemed excited, his nose only an inch from Guppy's face.

'Do you know,' said the big man, 'you can make wine out of anything, even old boots, if you've got sugar and yeast. That's true. That's true. Anything in this world that had a bit of life in it once. Of course, it would probably taste like boots, so there's not much point, but it still illustrates something, doesn't it?'

'Dead rats?' grinned Guppy, getting in on the joke.

Trader stared at him and Guppy was finding it difficult to focus on the other man's features, he was so close.

'Dead – rats . . . I don't *think* so. Not really. But certainly flowers – even weeds – and fruit of any kind. Honey, eh? We could try looking for some honey soon. What time of year is it?'

'Comin' on summer soon,' said Rupert, wiping his nose on one sleeve.

Trader looked thoughtful.

'Got a bit to wait then. Still, I'm glad I thought of it. Honey.'

I hope you remember it was your idea, thought Guppy, *when it doesn't work*. He had visions of this man pulling his head from his shoulders and using it to make wine. It wasn't a pleasant thought, for in such visions Guppy was never dead. His eyes in the severed head still looked out and saw, and what they would see was Trader bending over the pot, stirring with a big stick and saying, 'A little more honey, I think, ought to do it.'

'If I could get a few machine parts,' said Rupert, 'you wouldn't have to make any goddamn wine. We could be where those other bastards are, and drink what they're drinkin'. Oh, my. Just picture a bottle of bourbon . . .'

Guppy had no trouble with that and it hurt his feelings. He felt like crying. He felt as if someone he liked very much had just died.

Trader slumped in the armchair.

'So, what about you, my friend?' he said. 'What is your purpose in life?'

Guppy drew himself up. He had a mission too.

'I been tryin' to find a way out of the city.'

The other two looked at each other.

Then Trader asked, 'Did you? Did you find a way out?'

Some of the self-importance left Guppy's body and it went slack.

'Not yet,' he said.

Trader winked at Rupert and then reached inside his jacket, producing a large folded piece of paper. He knelt down and spread this paper out until it covered half the floor space. It was a mass of lines and words and Trader pointed to somewhere just left of the middle.

'You are here,' he said.

Guppy gaped.

'Am I? Where?'

'It's a map,' explained Rupert, carefully stepping around the piece of paper to stand by Guppy. 'Trader found it. It's a map of the city. There's nothing else. It goes on forever, see?'

Guppy stared at the tightly packed squares, lines and symbols, at the vastness of the streets, the giant maze. He could see that it was impossible to walk out of the city. It was too big.

It covered the whole world. You would die before you even got to the edge, wouldn't you? But there was a big space towards the top of the map. He pointed to it.

'Maybe that's where out of the city is?' he said. 'Maybe the city's grown round what's left of the outside?'

Rupert leaned forward, interest in his expression.

'What's it say there, Trader?'

The big man ran a finger underneath a word.

'*Airport*.'

'Where they have airplanes?'

Trader nodded.

'We got to go there,' announced Rupert, emphatically. 'I can get some stuff there to make a space ship. Then we can go where the other bastards have gone.'

Trader shook his head.

'It was a holocaust. I keep telling you.'

Guppy blinked. Words he didn't understand always made him blink. Rupert obviously understood, because Trader had discussed it with him before. Guppy heard Rupert say, 'No bombs!'

15

Guppy repeated the words. 'No bombs.'

'That's what I said,' cried Rupert, triumphantly. 'My old man had a job when I was a kid, fixin' automobiles. He used to let me help him with the wirin'. I reckon I remember enough to make something that'll get us off the ground.'

'What happened to your old man?' asked Guppy.

'Oh, he died.' Rupert seemed reluctant to expand on that, but said, 'I found some old wrecks in my time, but the works is always tore out. You got to get things that have kept on going since then – like one of them street cleaners.'

'Maybe at the airport?' suggested Guppy.

Rupert's eyes shone. 'Yeah.'

Trader said, 'I never knew my old man. I was on a boat with my mom and we seemed to go from place to place, and I remember no one would let us in. Kept turning us away. Then one day we just came into a place where there was no one left to turn us away. It was really quiet. There were cranes and big warehouses, but nobody working in them. Some of us started walking – I guess I must have been six or seven at the time – and two men came in the middle of the night. They took my mom away with them . . .'

There were tears in Trader's eyes and Guppy looked away and stared at a hole in the ceiling, where the lamp used to be.

Trader continued, 'I remember one of the other men with us kept looking round him and saying, "It must have been a holocaust." '

'A holocaust with no bombs,' said Rupert.

Trader's nostalgia turned to anger.

'I say yes,' he snapped.

' 'Titled to your opinion,' sniffed Rupert. 'Now how about something to eat? You got some beans?'

'I don't know what I've got 'til I open the can, do I? Give me a few minutes.'

Trader left the room and Rupert folded the map, saying, 'You got to let him be secretive. Otherwise he might take off with the whole lot. He don't keep it all to himself and that's all that matters.' He paused. 'What about this airport? You think we can get to it? Planes were just flying cars. I reckon if we could get our hands on a plane, we could get the hell out of here. Waddya say?'

'What about if all the parts is rotten?'

'I'm not saying we'll find one complete. But I could get some stuff out of one and put it in another, see? One of these days I'm gonna manage to catch one of them street cleaners. It all adds up.'

Guppy shrugged. 'I ain't got nothin' to do.'

'That's it then. We'll get to that airport if it kills us. Trader will come if I push him hard enough.'

The little man's ratty features were full of optimism and Guppy began to feel excited. Things were happening at last. There was something for them to do, which seemed like progress. It was a very attractive idea. One thing he still did not understand, and he put the question to Rupert.

'What made you ask me today? To come here?'

Rupert shrugged. 'You looked kinda lonely and lost – and I never felt we was complete, you know? Trader and me. Three is a lucky number. I heard that somewhere. All the things have got to fit together right, or they don't move at all – like a car, see? Some people are made to fit together, then they get things done. I dunno. All I know is I'm sick of just livin' around. Something's got to be done, and we've been bumming around too long. You need changes to make that happen . . .'

'Dynamics,' said Trader, re-entering the room.

'Yeah. Like that,' agreed Rupert.

Over the meal, which was some kind of pressed pink meat that tasted as if it had come straight from God's larder, Trader talked some more about his mother. He remembered her telling him that there would be motorbike gangs and groups of men with shotguns roaming the city. He had never seen that, had Guppy? No. Had Rupert? No. Funny, his mom had been so sure of it. Maybe it was one of them that took her away? He only remembered seeing two guys, in filthy clothes that he could smell from ten yards away, but it was dark and there could have been more waiting in the shadows. His mother had screamed abuse at first and then went quiet. Trader had been frightened and had run away and hid. When he came back, his mother and the two men were gone. He looked for her, but never found her.

'Maybe it was a bike gang?' he said, sucking meat between his teeth, 'but I didn't hear any bikes. I saw one or two around after that, but they didn't have any tyres on them and made a

17

noise on the road to wake the dead. I would've heard bikes, I think.'

It seemed important to him that his mother had not been kidnapped by the people she feared the most, so Guppy said, 'You would have heard bikes.'

Trader nodded. He seemed satisfied.

That night, just before Guppy fell asleep, Trader murmured, 'So your name's Guppy?'

'That's right,' said Guppy, softly, so as not to wake Rupert, who was already asleep.

'Guppy, Guppy,' said Trader, as if tasting the word, 'that's a fish, isn't it? Why are you called after a fish?'

'I didn't know – I didn't know it was a fish.'

'Well, it is.'

There was silence.

After a while, Guppy said, 'Goodnight Trader.'

But there was no reply.

Chapter Three

Rah, Rah, black rat
Have you any meat?
Yes, sir. Yes, ma'am,
Eat, eat, eat.

That night Guppy slept better than he had done in a long time. That's not to say he slept deeply, which could be achieved any time he had something strong to drink, but he slept soundly. There was a difference. The difference was in the waking – how you felt when you woke up.

He felt *good*. The day was full of hope, full of promise. Things were happening. For a start, the sunlight through the window looked a kind of brassy colour. It needed a polish, but it wasn't the murky stuff he was used to waking up to. Maybe the sun was different in this part of the city?

Guppy threw off the coat and rug that was keeping the warmth in, and went to the window. He looked out and saw that the world was much younger. There were people in the streets, hurrying to work. Cars went back and forth every few seconds and a newspaper vendor was waving his wares at passers-by. Overhead, an aircraft was moving slowly, very slowly, across the blue sky. It was nice. He could see customers in the eating place across the street, sipping at coffee and forking up eggs.

'Not in the house,' said a lump from the other corner of the room.

Guppy looked down, dismayed, and saw the pool on the floor. He had unconsciously been urinating. He pushed the flap of his fly in and hitched his pants.

'Sorry,' he mumbled.

'Outside's the place for that,' said Rupert.

'Yeah. Sorry.'

19

Rupert sat up. Without his coat he looked like a kitten that had been caught out in the rain. There was nothing of him worth mentioning to anyone interested in physical fitness.

'Don't matter. We're movin' on today,' said Rupert.

Trader was still asleep, snoring loudly.

The little man then asked, 'What was you lookin' at? Out there?'

Guppy moved away from the window to the centre of the room. He was embarrassed at being caught in one of his funny moods.

'Nothin'.'

Guppy had visions, occasionally, which he never told anyone about. He had seen people through the windows of houses, sitting around a table, playing cards or drinking. None of the men had beards and the women looked as though they were always laughing. There was a lot of furniture in these rooms.

He liked these sudden insights into a lost world. They softened the edge of life. But when the scenes were not there, it didn't bother him too much. It was no good trying to force them: they came and went as they pleased.

Once Trader was up and around, the day seemed to start properly. Trader went off somewhere and came back about an hour later. He called to them from the street and they went outside to see that he had a handcart covered with an old rug. Guppy knew there were cans underneath, but he didn't say anything.

Neither did Rupert, who went back into the house and came out with a length of metal pipe. He put it on top of the rug.

'Never know,' he said.

Trader nodded sagely.

'Can't be too careful.'

The trio set off, down the street, heading at an angle to the direction of the sun. Trader said it was north and Guppy believed him. They had to keep walking in open squares, because the main roads all seemed to go westward. No one complained.

At the end of one street they passed seven or eight kids: a gang who had somehow managed to trap a kestrel hawk and had wrung its neck. The kids asked if the men wanted to trade. A ginger-haired girl did the talking.

'What for?' asked Rupert.

Ginger said, 'Whaddya got in the cart?'

'Some old clothes. You want some old clothes?'

'Naw. You got somethin' else?'

'Only old clothes.'

The kids, the eldest of whom was not much more than ten years of age, looked disappointed.

'Shit. We'll just hafta eat the fuckin' bird.'

They watched the trio go past with something in their eyes that made Guppy glad that Rupert had thought to bring the metal pipe. But soon the place was behind them and the kids didn't follow.

At noon they came to a building which rose from the ground and went up into the clouds. It was the tallest building any of them had ever seen, they admitted to each other. Rupert had an idea.

'Why don't we go up to the top and see if we can spot the airport from there? Should be able to see for miles.'

Guppy was doubtful.

'It'll take us too long. Look how high it is.'

'So?' said Rupert. 'Even if we have to spend a night in there. So what?'

Trader nodded.

'It's a good idea. We don't know where the hell we're going at the moment. We could be heading in the wrong direction entirely. It's these streets – they go off at all angles.'

Guppy sighed.

'Okay, it's two to one. What about the cart?'

'I'll stay with the cart,' Trader volunteered generously. 'You two go up. When you get to the top, throw a stone over, so I know when you've made it. I'll wait here.'

Guppy said, 'I don't mind staying with the cart, if you want to go, Trader. You know what an airport looks like and I'm good at watching things.'

'Wouldn't dream of it,' said Trader, gripping his possessions. He looked like a man making an enormous sacrifice. 'I'll get to go up one of them one day. Don't you worry about me, Guppy.'

Guppy found himself being propelled through the doorless opening by Rupert's firm hands. The pair of them found the back staircase and began the climb. As they made their way towards the sky, they passed writings on the walls which neither of them could read. Sometimes there were pictures. Rupert kept pointing to them and saying, 'That ain't right. That just ain't right. Nobody's got one that size.' Or, 'I ain't never seen a woman with sharp ones, have you?' After a while he shut up, because he was out of breath and Guppy was glad for that.

The journey took forever. They just kept walking and resting, climbing and resting, until Guppy was afraid they would get too weak and not be able to go up or down. It made him panic, to think that he might die in a place so narrow, cut off from the rest of the world. Whenever he looked up, there were stairs ahead of him. Whenever he looked down, stairs again. The world was made of stairs and it had his head spinning.

'Maybe we ought to go back?' he suggested.

'Must be nearly there,' said Rupert.

But after he had said it for the sixth time, Guppy no longer believed him. At every turn of every floor, he felt that the next would be the top, but it never was. There was always another flight to go up, and then another, and another, until he really did feel sick and frightened. Where did they think they were going? There was nothing to find at the top anyway.

As they climbed, they passed filth and rubbish, the latter not of any worth. The wind blew in through broken windows and bothered Guppy with its constant tugging at his clothes and hair. It was cold, too, though he was used to that. What had he got himself into? Yesterday he would not have even considered such a foolish expedition.

They passed a dried corpse, giving it a wide berth. It had been there for a long time, its head tucked between its elbows, and its knees buried in its stomach, as if it had been trying to roll down the stairs like a ball, all the way to the street. It was crisp and flaky now and even the rats weren't interested.

Every so often, Guppy looked out of the window but the view was blocked by other buildings around them. They had to get higher, to get some long-distance airspace.

So the climbing continued, until Guppy suggested that they go through one of the doors to see what was inside the building. Rupert agreed and they took the next open doorway, leading off the stairwell.

There was nothing there but empty rooms.

They went back to the stairs.

Just as it was getting dark, they reached the roof. Tired and hungry, they found a room and lay on the floor. Neither of them had remembered to bring any food and it was best not mentioned. Guppy could feel the room swaying as he tried to get to sleep. It made him want to dig his fingers into the floor and hang on. He was so tense, he hardly slept at all.

As soon as it was light, they found their way out onto the roof.

Once outside, they were in another world. The rooftop covered about two acres, most of which was cultivated land, with cabbages and potatoes growing in neat rows. There were other crops too, including a couple of trees. In the middle of this was a square pool with white tiles, some of which were covered in algae. There were steps leading down into the pool. Around the edges of the roof were cages full of animals.

'Rabbits,' said Rupert, excitedly. 'Someone's caught rabbits and kept 'em in cages.'

He cupped his hands and yelled through them.

'HELLO!'

Guppy was nervous.

'Quiet. They might hear you.'

There was a small house on the roof which had been boarded up in places. A door opened and someone stepped outside. It was a woman wearing a coat of rabbit skins. Her hair was tied up behind her head with a piece of rag. She glared at them.

'We don't mean no harm,' said Guppy. 'We didn't know no one was here. We just come up from the street to look over the city.'

The woman folded her arms. She was small and tight, with a hard-looking jaw, and she seemed tough.

'This is my place,' she said.

Rupert stepped forward, smile as wide as a sunset, coat flapping like a swashbuckler's cloak, palms out in a placatory gesture.

'We know – leastways, we could see it belonged to *somebody*. You grow all this stuff yourself? My, that's really something. An' the animals too! Take a bit of caring for, I'll bet . . .'

'Come any closer,' she snapped, 'and I'll cut your heart out, you ratty little bastard.'

23

Rupert grinned. He didn't seem scared of her, though Guppy felt he ought to be. She looked a strong woman, despite her size, and though no knife was visible, Guppy bet it would only take a second to find one on her person.

Rupert nodded at the pool.

'You catch rainwater in that? Good idea.'

'It catches itself,' she said. 'What do you want? I can't spare much food. Even though it looks a lot, it's got to keep me . . .'

Both Guppy and Rupert snatched at the word 'much'. She hadn't said, 'no food', or 'any food' – which meant they were going to eat.

'Maybe just a bite,' said Rupert, with a gay little laugh, which Guppy felt the woman must find sickening. 'And maybe some water?'

'Then will you go?'

Rupert nodded, winking at Guppy.

'What was that for?' asked the woman.

'What?' Rupert was all wide-eyes and innocence.

'That look you gave your friend. You give me any trouble and I warn you, I won't think twice about killing both of you.'

Rupert drew himself up.

'Madam, I have no intention of giving trouble. Can I help if it I've got a cheerful disposition?'

Guppy guessed he must have heard that phrase from Trader, because it sounded foreign on Rupert's lips.

She went inside the little house and came out almost immediately with some vegetables on a piece of card. Then she stood over them while they ate it. Rupert kept glancing at the rabbits but he didn't say anything.

'That was nice,' he said, once they had eaten.

'Yeah,' added Guppy. 'Nice.'

They both drank from the pool. The water was a little scummy, but they could tell it was clean.

'What was this place?' asked Rupert.

'Used to be a swimming pool, with lawns around it. That there was the penthouse. Now it's my land. I own it.'

'Who says?'

'I've been here five years. That makes it mine. I had a man with me, but he died.'

'Was that him on the stairs?' asked Rupert.

'No, that was someone I had to stick with my knife. Caught them stealing rabbits. I threw my husband's body over the edge. He must be in the street somewhere.'

'Was he dead when you pushed him?'

Guppy thought Rupert's insinuation would make her angry, but she smiled and said, 'Just about.'

'So you're alone now,' said Rupert.

'I see people from time to time, when they've got something to trade.' She reached inside her coat and drew out a long-bladed knife. Guppy stared at it, then took a step back. Rupert stayed where he was, still grinning.

'You need some help round here? I could stay with you and give you a hand.'

She sneered at Rupert's suggestion.

'You think I need a *man*? I don't need a man. I do very well on my own.'

'That's true. I can see that. But I was thinking of just . . . you know, company. You play cards?' Rupert drew out a greasy tattered deck from his pocket. Many of the originals had been replaced by pieces of thin card marked with a pencil. 'Maybe we could play cards and talk and stuff like that? I get pretty lonely too, most days. You think this hick is good company?' he gestured towards Guppy. 'He don't know his ass from his elbow. Might as well make friends with a rabbit. You look an intelligent lady. I bet you know all kinds of card games. We could have a really elegant time.'

A hunger sprang into her eyes. Even Guppy could see it. A hunger for a companionship no longer available in a world where you could not even trust your brother or sister to keep tight company with you.

'Cards,' she murmured with a faraway look in her eye.

Rupert began strutting.

'Play all kinds of games. Bridge, rummy, blackjack, whist . . .'

'Whist,' she said.

'Especially whist,' said Rupert, 'though I'm not much good at it,' he added with a laugh. 'Get beaten a lot of the time, but I like to play. Oh, yes, whist is one of my favourite games.'

'You're full of bullshit,' said the woman, her face losing its dreamy look, 'but I like you. Why don't you stay a while. I can always cut your heart out if it doesn't work.'

25

'Why not?' laughed Rupert. 'If it doesn't work, I won't want to live anyway.'

She laughed too.

'Bullshitter.'

They went into the house together, still laughing, leaving Guppy alone and miserable.

Guppy yelled, 'Trader's waitin' downstairs, Rupert. He's waitin' for us now.'

Rupert came out of the house. He wasn't wearing his big overcoat and his arms poked out of the waistcoat holes like sticks.

'You go, Guppy,' he said. 'I ain't comin'.'

'But what about the space ship?'

'You build it. You'll be all right.'

'But it's you who's supposed to be doing that,' cried Guppy, getting angry. 'We don't know anything about it.'

Rupert snarled, 'Get off my roof, man. I don't want to see you up here again.' His eyes had narrowed to slits.

Guppy felt something go snap inside him and he shook his head. He stumbled towards the door to the stairs and without looking back, began to descend. It was much easier, going down, though he had to stop from time to time to get rid of the dizzy feeling. All he wanted to do was get to Trader and tell the big man what had happened. He wasn't sure whose fault it was, but he had an idea that Trader would blame him. He had never felt so cut out of anything before and it hurt that Rupert had rejected him.

When he reached the ground, Trader was nowhere to be seen. Guppy ran through the streets, yelling his head off, until he saw the black man stumble out of a doorway.

'What the hell are you yelling for, man? I was trying to sleep,' grumbled Trader.

'It's midday,' said Guppy.

Trader looked up at the sky.

'So it is. Where's Rupert?'

Guppy took three swallows and told Trader the whole story, at the end of which Trader licked his lips and said, 'Rabbits? Hell, I haven't had rabbit stew in an age. I guess I can wait a bit longer though. Let's go and put the water on to boil.'

'Ain't you going to fetch Rupert?'

'Me? Climb those stairs. You've got to be crazy.'

'But he's not coming back,' cried Guppy. 'I saw him. He's going to stay there with her.'

Trader went inside the doorway and there was an end to their conversation. Guppy thought he was being callous. He'd known Rupert for longer than Guppy, and Guppy felt the loss strongly. All their plans, too, dashed to the ground and shattered. Just when things had begun to look bright, they went dark again.

Not long after the water had begun to boil in the pot, Rupert appeared, a limp rabbit in each hand.

'I only took two,' he said. 'That's fair, ain't it? And I left the cards. We'd better move on tomorrow, case she comes after me. She's good with knives. Almost nicked my ear when I ran for the stairs – stuck in doorpost.' He chuckled. 'Some woman that. Pity I got to build my space ship . . .'

Chapter Four

Little Jack Horner
Sat in a corner
Making a meat-filled pie:
He put in a thumb,
A lip and a gum,
An ear and a bonny blue eye.

The rabbit tasted just as it should. They couldn't stop grinning at one another as they ate it, the fat running down their chins and into their beards. It was glorious. The meat just peeled away from the bone and melted on their tongues, and there was more than enough to fill them to satisfaction. They were very fat rabbits, fed on cabbage leaves and carrots.

'That was some feast,' said Trader, leaning back and looking at the other two.

Guppy nodded happily.

'Some feast,' he repeated.

Then Trader said, 'Well?'

He had an expectant look on his face and Guppy wondered what it was all about. He stared at Rupert, whose expression had suddenly changed from blissful contentment to a sort of wary craftiness.

'Well what?' said Guppy at last, unable to bear the look on Rupert's face any longer.

'Well, did you see the airport?'

Guppy's heart sank and he knew that his own face now reflected Rupert's.

They had forgotten to do the very thing they had climbed all those stairs for. Jesus, Trader was going to be mad. He wondered what a mad Trader looked like and the picture was not at all pleasant.

Rupert said, 'Mist. It was too misty. Couldn't see more'n half a mile. Ain't that right Guppy?'

Rupert went back to picking a legbone that hadn't got a shred of meat on it. Guppy's heart was racing.

'That's just it,' he said. 'Mist all over. Fog probably.'

Trader's brow knitted.

'Sun was shining all day.'

Rupert sighed. 'Yeah, I know. Probably responsible for kickin' up vapours from the river.'

'What river?'

'You mean you didn't see the river on the map? Cheez, I saw it, didn't you Guppy? Right up ahead of us. Big wide river like a blue snake.'

Guppy didn't know whether he answered Rupert's question the way he did because he felt it was more subtle to deny having noticed the landmark or because he knew that Trader's next action would be to check on the accuracy of the observation. He had both the sneak and the coward in him and it could have been either one.

'I didn't see that. No, I have to admit, I didn't see that.'

Out came the map and Trader pored over it in the firelight. Guppy kept noticing how big the black man's hands were. They could have wrapped themselves around Guppy's head and crushed it like an overripe apple, no problem. Rupert just leaned back on his elbows. He had a smoking twig in his hand and he was blowing on the spark at the end, making it glow. He looked as though he hadn't got a care in the world.

Trader looked up.

'Yes – the river's here all right. We have to cross it in the morning.'

Guppy let out an enormous sigh of relief and Trader looked at him sharply, so he feigned a belch.

'Rich,' he said, tapping his chest with his fist.

The map was folded again and Guppy knew he would live to see another dawn. He pulled his blanket around his shoulders and stared into the fire. It held his attention until the others were asleep.

That night, Guppy slept out on the steps. He always preferred the outdoors, even when it was cold. Buildings were invariably damp and made him chesty, made his bones ache. He looked up at the stars, wondering which was the one that all the people had gone to. What would they be doing on their new world? Having a good time, probably. Guppy had only a vague idea what a *new world* might look like: it was a place where people were fat, had no sores on their bodies and an endless supply of booze at their fingertips. As for the scenery, well that was sort of shiny – a silver haze of light – with no real shapes to define it. Warm though, and the sound of water in the background.

The bastards! Fancy leaving him behind. You couldn't credit the selfishness of some people.

He turned over on his side, thinking how wonderful it was going to be when they landed on such a place. Wouldn't the people be surprised to see them!

Suddenly, a string of lights appeared in the distance. Guppy watched them, winding their way through the night city, like an illuminated snake drifting between buildings. It was a train, moving silently through the darkness. Guppy listened for the rumble of the wheels on the track, but it never came, even though the train passed by quite close: near enough for him to see the passengers reading their evening newspapers or looking with bored expressions out of the windows. A conductor was making his way down the aisle, checking tickets, and a group of youngsters were laughing over some joke or other. The silent noise they were making was disturbing an elderly woman in the adjacent seat. Some of the passengers had their eyes closed, sleeping off a hard day at the office. None of them seemed concerned by what tomorrow might bring.

Guppy closed his own eyes and sleep came easily.

The following day the trio set out again. Mid-morning they came to a large building with pillars on either side of the huge entrance. It was an old place – at least it looked old – and it had writing over the doorway. Trader told them what it said.

'Museum,' he stated.

'What's one of them?' asked Guppy.

'Place where they used to keep old stuff that nobody could use any more. People would go and look at it.'

'What for?'

'See how their grandfathers did things.'

Rupert asked, 'Would there be machines in these places?'

'Oh, yes. Just about everything, so long as it was old.'

'Maybe I'll find something to help me with my space ship? Why don't we go look inside? You never know.'

The little man in the big coat floated up the steps and entered the museum. Guppy followed him, while Trader stayed outside with the cart.

The pair of them roamed through the museum, picking up things and dropping them. The whole place was a mess. There were bones lying around all over the place. Bones that made their rabbits look like the skeletons of insects in comparison. There were strange statues too, most of which had been pushed over by previous visitors and lay headless or limbless on the floor. All the useful stuff had obviously been taken, but they found one glass cabinet which had not been shattered. Rupert took care of that and reached inside to take out a small box with sandpaper edges.

'Well, look at this. 'Member what these is?'

Guppy had to admit he didn't.

'Matches. A box of matches.'

Now he remembered. Instant fire.

'Try one,' he said.

Rupert opened the box and took out one of the little sticks with the red heads. He tried to strike it along the sandpaper, but the red stuff just creamed off. He tried another with the same result.

He tossed the box away in disgust.

'Pity. We could've used that to start our fires, instead of messing around with that damn bow drill all the time. Matches would have been real quick.'

'You can't trust these old things. They've been here too long,' said Guppy.

'You're right about that.'

But they did find something useful: a set of metal wheels – large ones – from an old vehicle. They took them outside, to Trader, who inspected them. The cart only had small wheels, which were beginning to buckle under the weight of the cans and Trader was delighted at their find. He spent the next two hours modifying the axle to take the new wheels and then they started out again.

Around noon, they came to a department store which looked worth a search. Trader needed replacement footwear, since the shoes he wore were held together with bits of cord wound round to keep the soles attached to the uppers. Rags had then been wrapped around the cord to prevent wear.

Plastic boots were best since they didn't rot. Leather was useless. The stitching always came apart the moment you put them on.

They roamed through the store finding little of value. Trader happened across a case of rifles and shotguns, but as usual they were useless. Even if they could have found ammunition, which was unlikely, the barrels and firing mechanisms were rusted. Guppy admitted that he wouldn't have known how to work them anyway. Since he had met the other two, he realised how little he knew about anything.

'I'm a dippy,' he said to Rupert.

'Naw. You just forgot things. You been boozin' so long it's made your brain soft. That don't mean you're stupid, do it? Stupid is when you pretend to know everything, and don't know shit.'

He felt a bit better after that.

Before they left, Trader set a few snares for rats, in case they came back that way again. Rupert scorned the idea since he reckoned on being out in space soon, on his way to the place where the others had gone. Guppy didn't know what to think but didn't see any harm in investing in the future.

'You never know what's going to happen,' he said.

The way Rupert spoke about leaving earth, always had Guppy's chest filling with hope. The little man's enthusiasm and optimism were contagious. Guppy could have listened to him chattering on for hours, if Trader didn't keep shutting him up. There were times, however, when he had one or two doubts about Rupert's expertise.

'How come you're so good at mechanics when you can't even read?' he asked.

Rupert was unabashed.

'I told you, my old man was the best. He taught me everythin' he knew. I could take a trash can and make it fly. It's all in here.' He tapped his head. 'It's a natural gift. My old man worked on cars, airplanes, you name it. You see, round about the time the bastards abandoned us, technology – that's the stuff all about machines – was bang up to the mark. Engines came all wrapped-up in plastic, the size of a shoe box, and all you had to do was fit a wire here, and a wire there, to make the thing go. Nothin' to rust, because it was all sealed in. Nothin' to go wrong, really, except that nothing is go-wrong proof, no matter how simple or protected it is. When we get to the airport, Trader can read any instructions for me, on the labels. I'll fit 'em together. Trust me.'

Guppy trusted him.

Trader said, 'How come the guns don't work?'

'Because they're old-fashioned technology, is why.'

'How come there are no cars working?'

'Because they stopped making 'em and people used the ones that were around until they wore out. Anyway, they probably took the best ones with them. You only see old wrecks around here.'

'Maybe they took all the flying machines too?'

'Maybe they did, maybe they didn't. It was all done of a rush to my way of thinking. Everybody that was in the know went to the airport and took off. Them that didn't, like us, never got to the airport because . . . because we wasn't informed enough. Could be that our space ship is still waitin' for us. If not, we'll find the bits to make one. See, if you think about it enough, the airport was the place where everythin' was at – there at the end. They was bound to leave some bits behind at the last place they left.'

Guppy thought this sounded reasonable, but he still had one remaining question.

'Why did they go?'

Rupert looked exasperated. He gestured at the scene around them: the cracked and crumbling streets, the collapsing buildings, the piles of rubbish and shells of cars.

'Well *look* at it. The place is falling to pieces. Would *you* want to stay here?'

'No, but . . .'

'There it is then. We know where we got to go. We know what we got to do. All that's to be said, is said.'

That night it rained hard and they spent the time in a building occupied by an old man. They took over a room on the ground floor and they could hear the old man moving about above them. Every so often he came down the stairs and peered in at them, probably hoping to catch them eating. The old man looked thin and wasted, with some kind of disease: his skin coming off in flakes. Guppy was glad he didn't come into the room.

Guppy thought about what Rupert had stated. The fact that there was no more to be said. That wasn't true. There were always questions to be answered. People were full of questions, clogged with them. When someone you met in the street didn't ask you a question right off, it wasn't because they had none in them, it was because they had so many they were constipated with them. Guppy hadn't met a person yet who had no questions left inside them. Rupert was choked with them, but he didn't need the answers from anyone else. He always answered them himself: that way he got the reply he wanted. Probably Rupert couldn't afford to be wrong or he would just crumple up, fold away into the dust and never move again.

During the night they took it in turns to stay awake. The old man's skin condition reminded Guppy of the sores that covered his chest and back. While the others were asleep, he took off his clothes and inspected the open wounds. They were running with pus and it frightened him. He took a wet rag and cleaned them up the best way he could, by the light of the moon coming through the window. He didn't want the others to see them.

Once, the other occupant of the building came down and stood in the doorway, whispering, 'Eh? Eh? Eh?' over and over again. Guppy made shooing motions and eventually growled at the old man like a dog. The man scuttled away, up the stairs again, to pace the floor for the rest of the night. Guppy was able to concentrate on his body once more and while his shirt was off, got rid of a few lice that infested his pubic hair. He enjoyed the crack of the little bodies when he nipped them between thumb and forefinger.

Then he dressed again, feeling he had accomplished a great deal. He wished he had a drink of some kind. If they could find some sugar for Trader, or even some honey, he would be able to make them some wine. *Wine* sounded wholesome. It was not like cleaner fluid or even whisky. Wine did you good. It was full of things that satisfied the corners of your body, as well as your head.

Later, he woke Rupert, who took over from him.

When he opened his eyes again, it was daylight and Trader was trying to get a fire going, but the wood, even the door strips from inside the building, was damp from the night's rain and it was an impossible task.

The old man came and threw a rock into the room, before racing upstairs, shouting something incomprehensible. Rupert wanted to chase him but Trader said to leave him alone.

'He's dying. You got to make allowances.'

'We better get out before we catch what he's got,' said Guppy.

'Yeah,' agreed Rupert. 'I already got this kidney. Pissed a bucket of blood this morning.'

'Men come and go,' said Trader, 'but disease abides.'

Guppy thought that was a peculiar thing to say, but he didn't tell Trader that. Instead, he had a sudden desire to confess.

'I – I got these sores,' he said.

'Huh!' said Rupert, staring hard at him. 'Who the hell ain't? I got a crater on my arse you could drop a brick down an' not touch the sides.'

So, that was that. Guppy was happy once more. He looked out of the window. A man hurried past, his trench-coat collar up to protect his suit from the rain. There was a pipe in his mouth, gripped firmly between his teeth, and a kind of savage expression around his lips and eyes, as if rain were the worst kind of hell a man could experience on this earth. Guppy said, 'Hi,' but the figure turned the corner, just as the pipe-smoker glanced at his wristwatch, like a man with seconds on his mind.

Guppy didn't even know what minutes were and was barely familiar with the hours.

On the way to the river, they came across a still-smoking fire, with charred human bones in its ashes. Some of them were the arm and legbones of a child.

'Cannibals,' said Trader, looking round at the buildings.

Guppy felt a chill go through him. Those groups who had fallen to the level of eating human flesh tended to inhabit small pockets of the city. If you stumbled across such an area, you were lucky to escape whole. It wasn't the fact that they were cannibals that bothered Guppy, but the knowledge that they kept humans like cattle, and slaughtered them for the meat. It

35

was known that many such groups would keep their victims alive, even after amputating limbs, so that the bulk of the meat could be kept fresh. The last pieces of a body, to go down those throats, were the soft meats – the offal – and Guppy could well envisage his swollen liver sizzling on the end of a pointed stick.

'I don't like it here,' he said.

Rupert said, 'Who the fuck does?' Then he yelled at the surrounding buildings, 'There's three of us! Three fit men. Anyone who tries anything'll get hurt bad. We'll take some of you with us . . .'

There was a distorted answer, an echoing reply, from somewhere in the derelict apartment blocks. It was like a moan from the earth. Then a wild, savage face appeared at one of the windows, only to disappear again quickly.

'We're goin' now,' shouted Rupert. 'Anyone who tries to follow us, we'll cut him open like a dog. We'll see who eats who, anyone follows – you got that? I got a mind to chew on somebody's eyeballs, myself . . .'

The trio walked down the street, Rupert glancing behind them occasionally, and Guppy and Trader watching the sides. It took an incredibly long time to get into more open areas.

Once they were clear, Guppy almost collapsed.

'I *hate* those places,' he said, unnecessarily. 'I met a man who once had his hand ate, but got away later. He said these people got hard white eyes – you know, like stones – an' you can tell 'em from a long ways off . . . see that guy that came up at the window. He looked like that.'

Trader cleared his throat before saying, 'Hate to disappoint you, Guppy, but I don't think he was a cannibal.'

Guppy didn't understand.

'What was he then?'

'I think he was the one they were eating.'

Chapter Five

Star light, star bright,
Warming planets in the night,
That's the place where we must go,
Leave the others, down below.

The two men in the neat white spacesuits stepped from the shiny craft onto the surface of the new planet. One of them pretended to trip over as he jumped from the bottom rung of the descent ladder. The other grabbed his arm.

'You okay, Joe?'

'Yeah,' Joe grinned. 'Didn't realise it was such a large step.'

Al winced. 'Christ, that's corny.'

They both stood there for a moment, staring out over the new world. The purple plains stretched before them, under a magenta sky. Bright yellow trees swept upwards on the slope of the distant mountains from which ran a narrow green river fringed by tall reeds.

'Pretty much as we expected,' said Joe. He stuck a stick with a flag at the top, into the turf at his foot.

'How about we put the city right here?'

'Looks good to me. You want to call the others?'

Joe said, 'Wait a minute.'

He reached up and began to remove his helmet. The other man attempted to stop him, but Joe pushed Al off and eventually the helmet was in his hands. He breathed deeply and with a satisfied expression on his face.

'Smells of lilacs,' he commented.

'That was a pretty stupid thing to do Joe,' said Al.

'Naw. I was betting on a sure thing. You see those yellow antelope? They're oxygen-breathing creatures. I knew what I was doing.'

'What about bacteria?'

'We got to take our chances – but, you know, I got a feeling that this world is cleaner than the one we left. It's untouched, like a second Eden. This is paradise, man. We've made it.'

The second man then removed his own helmet and did a little skipping dance across the purple grass. When this ritual was over, he came back to Joe.

'Nice springy turf. We could put the football stadium right here and build the city round it.' He paused, then said, 'What's the matter?'

Joe said, 'I was just thinking of those poor fuckers we left down on Earth. Poor bastards – stuck in those crumbling cities – nothing to eat but rats. Don't you feel a twinge of conscience?'

Al hung his head for a moment.

'Yeah. Pretty lousy thing to do – leave them behind.' He continued to stare at the ground for a moment. 'All those rats, and the buildings coming apart.'

There was a sound like a stifled snigger following this statement and Al began to choke. He looked up at Joe, his face suffused with suppressed laughter.

Joe's mouth twitched. 'Aw, cut it out, Al.'

Al exploded into mirth. Joe followed his example, unable to contain the spasms of hilarity. They couldn't look at each other after that, without fresh guffaws bursting forth.

'Jesus, if we could have seen their faces . . . when they found we'd gone . . .'

Al shrieked with laughter.

'We're out of control, Joe.'

The tears ran down Joe's cheeks.

The river was swollen with the recent rains and debris clogged the banks. They stared first at the fast flowing water, cloudy with scoured mud, and then at the suspension bridge, hanging from one side so that the road was on its edge, dangling just above the turbulence.

Guppy said, 'I can't swim.'

'No way anybody could swim across *that* river,' announced Trader.

'What about we make a raft?' suggested Rupert.

'Get swept away,' replied Trader. 'Look at the speed it's going. We'd end up in the sea. Be drowned for sure.'

They walked along the concrete bank for a few yards, each of them lost in his own thoughts. The metal wheels of the cart made a grating sound on the path. The air was full of carking gulls.

'If only we could fly,' said Rupert.

But they couldn't, so there wasn't much point in pursuing that line of thought. Guppy tried to stir the sludge in his brain, but nothing came up from the bottom. It would have been wonderful if *he* could have come up with an idea to cross the river. The other two would have looked at him with new respect in their eyes. So far he hadn't done very much to help. If only the booze hadn't killed off half his thinking matter!

'Guess we'd better ask somebody,' said Rupert at last. 'You better let me handle it. I know how to deal with these things. What can you spare, Trader?'

'Nothing,' answered the big man, stopping his cart and stepping in front of it to protect its contents.

'Come on. Come on,' shouted Rupert. 'This is an emergency. There's got to be something in there we don't want.' He pushed Trader aside and rummaged under the rug, coming out with a thin, flat oval tin.

'This is the smallest. We'll use this.'

Trader's face grew thunderous and Guppy walked away a few yards.

'That's my favourite,' snarled Trader.

'Well, you choose one.'

Trader lifted the rug on the cart and began counting. He started over about three times, each time throwing Rupert an angry look, as if it were the little man who was interrupting his calculations. Finally, he looked at the flat tin in Rupert's hands.

'That one,' he said. 'That's the can.'

Rupert blew out his cheeks.

'Right. That's settled then. We got to find someone who knows the way across. You two stay here – I'm going to see who lives along the river.'

Rupert put up his coat collar and walked towards the buildings that lined the river, shouting over his shoulder, 'Stay put. I'll be back.'

Guppy went back to where Trader was standing and helped him spread the rug back over the top of the cart. Then the pair of them sat down by a parapet, out of the wind, to await the return of Rupert.

Sometime later, Rupert came back with a tall, lanky youth in tow. He introduced the newcomer to the others.

'This is Jamie,' said Rupert.

Jamie said, 'Hup!' in a flappy-lipped voice.

He was a seedy-looking kid with fluff on his chin and a mass of thick fair hair, which disappeared down into the hole of the blanket he wore. He had no shoes and his toes were each separated by a thick wad of grime. Jamie's mouth was torn at one side and hung down, revealing stained, yellow teeth from which the gums had retreated.

'How'd you hurt your lip?' said Guppy. Injuries always fascinated him. The instant he saw some wound or physical disfigurement, he imagined how it would feel to own it.

'Got it hookered – nayle,' Jamie replied. He kept twitching as he talked and he didn't seem to be able to look anyone in the eyes for more than a brief second.

'You stay around here?' said Guppy, indicating the buildings behind them.

Jamie nodded, his eyelid working furiously.

'Bin here since I was bored. Got a rack over,' he jerked his head sideways. 'Pickin' take ain't so feverish, comin' on now, but it'll spread.'

Guppy's head spun. 'Right,' he said, completely at a loss.

'How are you going to get us across the river,' asked Trader, getting down to practicalities.

Jamie looked at the can in Rupert's hand.

Rupert said, 'When we get across. Then you get it.'

The youth shrugged inside his blanket. It seemed to be full of pointed sticks.

'Sub's blocko. Bunged her up since the hot streets gone – but there's a pipe. I know her.'

He shuffled off, indicating that they should follow him.

'Better take my steps to use,' he called.

They trailed after him as he led them along the edge of the river. The walk was a long one and Guppy began to wonder whether they were being led into some kind of trap – an ambush – but eventually they came to a place where an open manhole lay. The youth called Jamie climbed down, into the darkness.

40

Rupert followed him while the other two waited at the top. There was a kind of echoing talk which went on down below, then Rupert reappeared.

'Can't see a damn thing,' he said. 'We got to get a fire going and make some torches.'

This proved more difficult than it sounded. They did manage to start the fire with Trader's expertise on the bow drill, but the torches proved to be more of an elusive task. Then the youth suggested scraping some of the tar from the surface of the road and using a piece of the rug on the cart. They transferred the fire to the gutter and managed to melt some of the asphalt. A piece of rug torn from the cart cover was rubbed in this until it was thick and black. With some wire, they tied the wadge to a stump of wood and then set it alight. It burned well, though with a stream of black smoke.

Jamie insisted, in his peculiar use of language, that his work was over. He didn't want to cross the river with them. He had shown them where it was, now it was up to them. The pipe – tall enough to take an average-sized man – went under the river to the other side. There was some water in it, but only ankle deep. He said he knew it went all the way over because he'd used it himself. He wouldn't 'skug' them on that. There wouldn't be any point. Rupert knew his 'rack' and they could come looking for him if the pipe proved to be blocked, like the subway.

They gave him the can and then Rupert went down the hole again, calling for Trader to lower the cart to him. Trader did as asked, though they found they had to remove the wheels first, and the three parts had to be passed down separately.

Guppy held their source of light and while the other two were fitting the wheels back on the cart, he looked down into the concrete tunnel along which they were to travel. It was frightening. The shadows from the torch danced for only a few yards along the smooth walls, running with water, before returning, quickly. There were echoing sounds: drips, clicks and splashes. The air was stale and musty.

'Hold that damn thing over us,' grumbled Rupert. 'Can't see nothin' while you're wavin' it about like that.'

'Sorry,' said Guppy. The smoke was making his eyes stream. A rat ran over his foot and instinctively he flipped it high in the air and stamped on it as it hit the floor. He held it there, struggling, under his heel.

'Keep that damn light still!'

'Got a rat,' he whispered, afraid of the echoes. He pressed down harder, until the wriggling stopped.

The wheel was on at last and Guppy picked up the rat – a plump one – by its tail. He put it under the edge of the rug, hoping the other two would be pleased with his efforts, once they were out of their present circumstances.

All three men peered down the huge pipe, seeing only as far as the light from the torch would allow. The darkness beyond was like a black wall.

'C'mon, let's go,' said Rupert. 'The smoke from that thing is getting up my nose. We got to get a move on, or it'll run out.'

But none of them wanted to be first to step into that concrete throat leading to an inner night. There was something about going into a round tunnel that stirred a subconscious fear in Guppy. Had it been square, he felt sure he could have accepted it more easily, but the way the walls curved up to meet at the top aroused a kind of terror. He wanted a crap, but he knew the others would be impatient with him. So he tried to think of something else. His buttocks tightened with the effort of trying to divert his thoughts.

'I'm . . .' he stepped inside the pipe, the water slopping over his feet, soaking the rags and then getting through to his boots. It was slippery underneath and the curved floor made it difficult to hold his balance. He couldn't use the edges of the pipe for support, because they were too far away.

He held the torch high to keep the smoke out of his eyes and called to the others. He heard the cart moving behind him, and Rupert said, 'I'll push – you pull.'

Guppy didn't like the noise of the wheels in the hollow place. It was like shouting blasphemies in a cathedral. It seemed wrong, though you couldn't say why. The deeper they went, the more steep the slope became, and the water dripped from the ceiling, hissing in the flame. Guppy knew that if the torch went out, he would go insane with terror.

It went out, sizzling under a stream of water.

Blackness. Guppy went rigid. He filled his pants, instantly. The tunnel began bouncing with screams that made him gasp for breath. He fell to his knees and began crawling, scrambling through the water, as fast as he could go. Someone clambered over the top of him and he struggled with this unknown person in the pitch darkness. Thankfully the screaming stopped but the terror didn't go away. He kept crawling, crawling, until at last he could see a dim light in the distance. A figure kept blocking this out, as it bobbed in front of him.

When he finally reached the source of the light, Rupert was there, waiting for him. Both men were sucking air with noisy mouths. They just stood there, looking up at the light, unable to climb out because the iron rungs to the ladder were missing.

They waited.

Some time later, Trader came out of the end of the pipe, hauling his cart after him. He was breathing hard but seemed otherwise unperturbed.

'You left me,' he said, accusingly.

Rupert said, 'I was just making sure it was all right. Someone had to go first, to make sure.'

Guppy was trembling. He went away from the other two to drop his pants and wash his backside in the water. When he had finished, he felt elated. He tied his pants again and joined his companions.

'We made it,' he said.

'No thanks to you two,' grumbled Trader.

Rupert said, 'It don't matter. Guppy's right, we got here. That's what counts. We're across the river. We can do that, we can do anythin'. Cheez, we're some heroes, you know? Not many people could do somethin' like that. We're the best there is.'

He shook hands gravely with the other two.

'I'm glad to know you,' he said.

'Fuck you,' replied Trader ungraciously, as Rupert was wiping his hand on his coat and looking at Guppy with a puzzled expression.

Rupert said, 'Gimme a bunk up, Trader.'

The big man picked him up and almost threw him out of the hole, into the open air. As this was going on, Guppy saw the rug move on the cart and a moment later the rat slipped out from underneath and made its escape, back into the darkness of the pipe.

Chapter Six

Four-and-twenty blackbirds
Baked in a pie
Gave me chronic dysentry
And now I'm going to die

Once the cart had been dismantled and was on the surface, Guppy prepared himself to be lifted up by the others. However, just as he was about to call them, to give him their hands, a sound came from the darkness of the tunnel. At first Guppy thought it was the revived rat, but then it sounded like something much bigger.

'Who's there?' he asked nervously.

'Don't you know me?' said a voice from the tunnel.

'Who's that?' he cried, though the voice sounded vaguely familiar. He was not afraid of it, which surprised him a little.

'It's me – your father.'

The tone was hollow.

'My father's dead.'

'Yes – but you wanted to talk to me, didn't you Guppy? Why else would you come down here?'

'To get across the river?'

'No. To talk to me.'

For a moment Guppy was silent, then he said, 'I just want to know what happened.'

The voice sounded sad, melancholy.

'I know. That's why you came to visit me. Well, I can't tell you a great deal, son. Only what happened to me, after I left your mother. You were just two years old then. I went north, just as you're doing now, but I was looking for work. I felt if I could find someone to take me on, I could send for you and your mother. It was a long road . . .'

'You abandoned us.'

'No, I was going to send for you.'

'Yes.'

'I went north. There were others like me. Thousands. We set out in old vehicles, some of them held together with nothing but dirt and spit. There was hope amongst us though and we started out singing, thinking we would be bound to find what we were looking for in the north of the city.

'It was cold. The winter was just putting its foot in the door, jamming it open, and it was already spouting about how pretty the snow would look, as it drifted down and settled in the parks, and how icicles and frost sparkled like precious stones. I'd heard it all before.

'After two days we came to road blocks – the inhabitants of that section of the city did not want us – and we had to make a wide detour.

'The next area was almost deserted. Someone said they had gone south, looking for the same thing we were after. We shook our heads at that and said that they were damn fools, since we'd heard that all the work was to be had in the north. We kept on going.

'The further north we went, the colder it got. Clouds were a kind of gunmetal blue, with pinky edges. There was no end to them. It got depressing after a while, just lying in the back of the truck, watching them roll over us, rushing after those people that had headed south.

'When the trucks ran out of fuel, we got out and walked. I was up front, son, encouraging the others. You'd have been proud of your old man.

'We ate what we could find in the gutters, which wasn't much, and begged some. Some of the men began dying, of dysentry and hunger. Some of the women, of hopelessness. At one place, they came out and fired on us with guns, but those who did the firing looked as desperate as we were and I just felt sorry for them.

'Finally, we came to a high, chainlink fence, which stretched across the city as far as you could see, on either side. There were spikes and barbed wire on the top of the fence and we could see more barricades behind it. At points along the fence were concrete walls manned by armed soldiers.

'I called to one of them and asked him why we couldn't go any further. He told me it was a concentration camp. I said we needed work and couldn't we come inside the concentration camp to look for it.

'He said, "You *are* on the inside. If you try to get out, I'm going to have to shoot you."

'That night I went out, into the street, and froze to death. I don't think anyone even bothered to bury me, so if you should see me lying around, son, do me the honours. I'd be very grateful . . .'

Guppy listened for more and a voice said, 'Are you comin' up, or what?'

Guppy jumped backwards, alarmed, as two sets of hands reached down for his face.

'Hey, Guppy. Wake up!' said Trader's voice from above.

Guppy raised his arms and allowed himself to be lifted out, into the day. He sat on the edge of the hole. He felt very weary.

'Can we go somewhere and sleep now?'

'Good thinking,' said Trader.

The landscape was an eerie wasteland of rubble and timber, with stunted trees growing from low angular hills. In the far misty distance was a skyline of buildings, but between the river and these was difficult terrain over which the cart would not be able to travel. It was an area of open stillness which filled Guppy's heart with misgivings, since he had never before been confronted by a far horizon. Even the sky looked bigger.

'Told you,' sniffed Trader. 'Holocaust.'

Rupert said, 'Nah. Flood more likely. Foundations crumbled, I bet.'

'What are we goin' to do?' asked Guppy.

Rupert said, 'Look for somethin' to carry the cans. A sack or some kind of bag. Must be somethin' around here. Trader, you better stay with the cart. Me an' Guppy'll go and look. Okay?'

'Okay by me.'

Guppy wasn't so sure.

'Are we going each alone?'

'Best way,' said Rupert, and the little man's hands disappeared into his huge pockets as he went away whistling some unidentifiable tune. Guppy took the opposite direction, apprehensive about wandering out into the unknown. He had never been north of the river before and he didn't like the look of it. It was much too quiet for a start and, as always in piles of rubble, there was the chance of falling through a hole and not being able to get out again.

He began walking through the valleys, between the mountains of bricks, turning over slabs and other objects in the hope that there was something underneath.

Gradually, his courage returned to him and he began to venture further into the interior. It was not a place likely to have many people, so there was a good chance of finding something useful. He climbed a stack of girders that formed a giant frame, to get a better view of the world.

To the south lay the river, still tumbling eastwards. To the north the buildings, beyond the undulating sea of bricks. A daytime moon was out and he gazed at its ghostly, pale form in the purple sky. It looked good enough to eat.

He descended the frame and began picking his way amongst the debris again, until he saw just what he was looking for: a huge piece of canvas, lying on the side of an escarpment.

The canvas was nailed to a beam of wood and formed a flap over a cave. He threw back the flap and peered inside the hole. In the dim light he could make out the shape of a bed and other pieces of furniture.

'Hello? Anybody home?' called Guppy.

There was no reply and he entered the cave cautiously, in case the occupants were about, but out of earshot. He inspected the interior. The bed was in good condition: an old iron frame wrapped around with ropes and strips of rag to form the springs. Stacks of printed paper had been spread on top of this, to make a mattress. It looked very comfortable.

At the back of the cave he made a discovery: large slabs of concrete had been fitted into the wall to form shelves, and these were filled with rusting cans of food. Guppy made a quick, anxious search for anything that looked like booze, but found nothing which might satisfy that inner craving which had been bothering him more than ever of late. He slipped one of the cans into each of his coat pockets and then looked around the rest of the place.

There was a broken mirror lying against one wall and a set of mouldy books that had been stacked to form a chair. He went back to the bed and lay on it for a few moments, indulging in a luxury he had not experienced in a long time. He undid the rags around his boots and pulled them off to inspect his sores and blisters. There was a bowl of water on the floor. He washed each foot in it in turn and used some paper to wipe them dry.

'This is a snug nest,' he said to himself. 'Maybe whoever lived here has gone away? We could spend some time here.'

However, he did not like the look of all that food on the shelves. Surely, if the owner had been gone a long time, then others would have looted the store. And why leave such a treasure in the first place, unless the owner had died, while out of his house?

Maybe it was the cache of a foodcan diviner? There were those who went around with their arms stretched out and their eyes closed, until their fingers started trembling at the tips. Then they would start digging. Sometimes they dug and dug and found nothing, but they said that was because the food was too deep to get at. Sometimes, though, they found cans in piles and left a marker which only they would recognise. It wasn't wise to carry a lot around with you, since others would soon latch on to you for shares.

The more Guppy thought about it, though, the more this cave seemed like someone's permanent home.

'Maybe I'd better get the others,' he mumbled. 'Trader'll know what to do.'

He was just pulling his boots back on when he heard a noise in the doorway. He looked up, startled, and let out a kind of 'uhhhhh' sound, as someone blocked out the light to the cave with their body.

The figure entered.

He was a big man: bigger even than Trader. In his right hand he carried an iron bar. A mass of black hair covered his face,

48

while on top he was completely bald. It was as if his head had been divided into day and night.

One of his eyes was missing and the lids had been sewn together with dark thread. The remaining blue eye stared at Guppy with astonishment lodged in its pupil.

The iron bar fell to the floor with a clatter and the two thick-fingered hands reached out to lift Guppy onto his feet. He was speechless with terror as the hands roamed over his body, pinching his flesh here and there as if testing for something. Then the big man grunted and threw Guppy bodily into a corner.

Guppy lay where he was, bruised and shaken, not daring to move. The other man walked around his home, checking on his personal items as if with a mental inventory. When he came to the shelves he surveyed the cans, his eye running along each line with meticulous precision. Finally he stopped, came to Guppy again and felt in his pockets, removing the stolen goods.

'I was goin' to put them back,' cried Guppy. 'I thought they was nobody's.'

The giant took no notice. Acknowledgement that someone had spoken did not even register in his eye. He merely placed the cans in exactly the same positions that they had previously occupied, so that even the rust patterns faced the same direction as they had before Guppy removed them.

Guppy fully expected that the next move would be to crush his head with the iron bar, but the giant carried on his domestic chores as if Guppy were not present. At one point, when the big man's back was to him, Guppy crawled slowly towards the flap, but any hopes about the man being deaf were quickly dispelled, as he casually turned, picked up the rigid Guppy, and threw him back into the corner again.

'What do you want with me?' cried Guppy.

There was no answer. A fire was lit, the smoke finding its way out of the top of the cave, through the loose brickwork. A solid-wood door was then pulled from a recess and jammed up against the exit with a beam of wood. The bottom of the post was kicked hard into place.

Then the owner of the cave punched open a can with a triangular piece of metal and sat on his bed, staring at the cowering Guppy. Once, during his short meal, he got up and pinched Guppy's cheek, smiling at him. Then he went back to dipping his fingers in the can again. The stale air and smoke in the room made Guppy feel heavy-headed and eventually he fell off to sleep.

When he awoke, it was dark. For a moment Guppy did not know where he was, though he realised he was in a warm and comfortable place, rather than in the open. Then he recalled his encounter with the giant and could hear breathing noises coming from the bed.

Guppy began to crawl across the floor in the direction of the exit. By degrees, he reached the beam that jammed the door. He wrenched at it. The beam stayed firmly in place. He heaved at it twice more, without making any impression.

Guppy crawled away, into the middle of the floor, banging his knee on the iron leg of the bedstead on the way. Then he felt around where the huge arm dangled over the edge of the mattress. Eventually he found the iron bar.

Guppy climbed carefully to his feet, lifting the metal bar. It was extremely heavy. He raised it up. It would take only one blow to cave that skull which gleamed in the dim light. But what if he should miss?

The iron bar was up. All he had to do was bring it crashing down. His hands began trembling.

He lowered the bar, feeling utterly miserable. He could not murder a sleeping man. It wasn't in him. He was hopeless when it came to violence.

The bar slipped from his grasp and clanged against the bed. Instantly, a hand gripped his shoulder and he felt himself being thrust across the room. There was a scuffling and then light entered the cave, as the door was removed and the canvas thrown back. The one-eyed man stared at him across the room as he blinked, unaccustomed to the light. He scuttled back into his corner and buried his head in his hands. A single kick from an unseen foot took all the breath out of his lungs. Then he was left alone.

He heard the man moving around the room, grunting to himself. Guppy stayed where he was, unwilling even to look up to see what was happening. He heard the sound of cans being moved. He peered through his fingers and saw the giant

50

prising the lid from a small round tin. Guppy knew what it was before it had been opened. A tin of polish.

The big man tasted the contents by dipping a finger into the polish and licking it. His face registered disgust and he looked about to throw the tin away, when Guppy shouted, 'NO!'

The giant stared at him.

'No,' repeated Guppy, 'I know what to do with it.'

Chapter Seven

Mary had a little pup –
She caught it in a pit.
She stuffed its gut with wild thyme
And cooked it on a spit.

Guppy gently prised the tin of polish from the hands of his captor and indicated that he would like the other to rekindle the fire. The big man did as he was asked, surprisingly docile, once given an order. Soon there was a small flame in the circle of bricks used as a grate. Guppy then set to work, separating the spirit from the polish, using the heat from the flame. At last he was going to get a drink!

Once he had the alcohol, he asked one-eye for something to mix it with, to make it last longer. Juice from a tin of pears was produced. The cocktail took only another few seconds to blend and then Guppy offered the can of booze to the giant man.

One-eye looked suspiciously at the tawny liquid. He stroked his bald head with the flat of his hand. He raised the can to his lips, staring at Guppy. Then he drank.

'You're going too fast,' said Guppy. 'Sip it, sip it.' He was desperate for a taste himself and it looked like the man was going to finish the whole can in three swallows.

There was a moment when the drinker's taste buds were obviously numbed by the alcohol. He had a blank expression on his face. Guppy smiled and nodded encouragingly. Then the giant's expression changed. His face went black with wrath and he sprayed the precious fluid in all directions, flinging the can against the wall.

'Aaeerraaahh!' he spat, reaching for the bowl of water in which Guppy had bathed his feet. He drank quickly. Then he gripped Guppy by the throat and began squeezing.

'Poison me,' he growled, speaking for the first time.

Guppy tried to explain, but the fingers around his neck were too tight to allow his words to come out. He struggled, ineffectually, against the terrible strength of the other man. His head began to swim and a black fog descended before his eyes.

Just at that point there was a shout from outside.

'Guppy! Guppy! Where the hell are you?'

The giant released his grip. Guppy sank to the floor.

He lay there for a few moments while the feeling returned to his throat and his head cleared. One-eye's back was to him. He jumped up, scuttled past the giant, and out of the doorway into the light. Below him, Rupert and Trader were roaming amongst the brickhills.

'Trader!' he screamed. 'Help me!'

The two men looked up in astonishment as Guppy went tumbling down the bricks to land at their feet. He grabbed Trader's legs for support.

'Help me,' he croaked. 'He's trying to kill me.'

He looked back and the giant man was leaping down the slope with his iron bar in his hand. He was surprisingly agile for one of his size. Trader remained motionless, but Rupert yelled and ran forward, flying through the air like a cat. He landed on the big man's chest, wrapping his legs around it and his hands clawed at the black-bearded face and remaining eye.

The giant screamed, managed to dislodge his assailant, and rolled away with the blood washing down his cheeks and beard. Then Rupert was up and running, shouting, 'Run away! Run, you bastards, run.'

Trader and Guppy were already flying over the bricks. Following them closely, came Rupert himself, coat billowing like a black cloak behind him.

There were shouts of anger from the rear. Huge slabs of concrete began landing around the trio. Had the thrower been just a little more accurate, one of them at least would have been crushed.

Rupert was howling with laughter as he ran, but whether this was nervousness, or whether he actually saw some kind of perverse humour in the situation, Guppy never did find out. His own terror was enough to keep his legs pumping and soon the sound of missiles landing amongst the debris was behind them. The roars of rage began to fade. They continued to put distance between themselves and the giant man.

'Mother of God,' said Trader, when they were able to stop for breath at last, 'you have some strange friends, Guppy. Where did you meet that one?'

'Wandered into his hole by accident,' wheezed Guppy. 'Wouldn't let me go. Think he was going to eat me. Kept pinching the fleshy bits and sticking out his tongue.'

'Christ,' said Rupert, 'how hard up can you get? I wouldn't eat you, you filthy bastard, if you was the last thing between me and starving.'

Guppy lay on his back and giggled, looking up at the grey clouds sweeping like a fleet of ships over their heads.

'Not hard up. Had a whole larder full of food. Saving me for last.'

Trader said, 'Let's get out of here before that guy finds us and eats us all.'

They went to the place where the cans were hidden and dug them out of the bricks. Trader had found a plastic suitcase – the kind that was ten times cheaper than leather when it was originally sold in the shops, but had lasted ten times longer. They took turns to lug the load, using the brick-sided valleys to circumnavigate the hills of rubble. It took them until evening to get clear of the area and into civilisation once again. The derelict buildings, with their damp plaster coming away in chunks, their gutters swinging dangerously in the wind, and their roofslates sliding down and skimming silently through the air, with the potential to decapitate, were infinitely preferable to the slag heaps of the south, with their hidden caves full of psychopathic giant cannibals.

'I can deal with *natural* dangers,' said Rupert. 'It's innatural things, like that bastard back there, scares me.'

'*Supernatural*,' corrected Trader. 'Or rather, *un*natural.'

'Abnatural, more like,' argued Rupert.

'You mean abnormal.'

'No, I mean unnormal,' refusing to be educated by someone who couldn't even take a little iron bar away from a half-crazed giant.

They rested for the night in the entrance to the subway. Trader told the other two that maybe the real people went underground, into the subway system below, and that was where the civilised community now lived.

'Whaddya mean, *real* people?' said Rupert. 'Are you in-sinsuatin' that I ain't real people?'

'I mean the ones with brains, like the scientists and the politicians. Some say they're down there now, having a hell of a time. They've got green grass down there, and cattle and engines working to fill the place with air. They got it made.'

Guppy said, 'I ain't seen nothin' of that.'

Trader retorted, 'Well, they're not going to let you know where they are, are they? They've only just got rid of bums like you. You think they want you fouling their clean air?'

That hurt Guppy, and he went all quiet and sulky for a while, leaving Rupert to argue with Trader.

'Where's the air shafts?' demanded the little man.

'Hidden from bums like you.'

'How come this bum, who's got ears just the same as *real* people, how come I can't hear the engines?'

'Yeah – well, they're quiet. Run by computers that just whisper a little.' Trader rustled a piece of paper, softly, to illustrate his point.

'They must come up sometimes.'

'They wear special white suits – you can't see them in the daylight.'

Rupert gave him a disgusted look, as if to say he knew that Trader was making it up as he went along and such stories didn't even deserve argument. Rupert tried another tack.

'These cattle then. What are they?'

Trader rolled his eyes.

'Mutant human beings. They keep them like rabbits and chickens, in cages.'

'Shit, this is a fairy tale. People in subways?' Rupert snorted. 'There's nothin' down there but stale air and rats . . .'

'And ghosts,' added Guppy.

Rupert stood up and walked into the interior of the subway, peering into the darkness, his coat making swishing sounds on the floor as it trailed after him. Then he returned to the fire.

'Gimme a light. I'm goin' in there to have a looksee.'

Guppy grabbed the hem of Rupert's coat.

'Don't do it. You don't need to prove nothin' to me Rupert. There's . . . terrible things down there.'

'You mean the banshee-howlers? Don't believe that neither. Gimme a light.'

He took a flaming piece of wood from the fire and began to walk into the tunnel. Trader yelled after him, telling him to come back or he would find himself in the cages with the rest of the mutants. Rupert took no notice, not even pausing to yell back at Trader that he wasn't a mutant either, which was what the big man implied. He disappeared from their sight.

Guppy looked reproachfully at Trader.

'You shouldn't have upset him. You know how he's got to prove you wrong all the time.'

Trader looked contrite.

'I know, I know. Something gets in me and I can't stop. He'll be all right. Won't he? We'll just sit here and wait for him to come out.'

While they sat and waited, a street cleaner went clattering past them, its bolts and joints squeaking. Guppy thought he ought to get up and chase it, to get some parts for Rupert's space ship, but he didn't want to leave the place in case his friend needed him. He told Trader they'd better not let on that a street cleaner had gone by, or Rupert would get mad that he wasn't there to go after it.

A little while later, Trader said, 'You think that guy – the one who had you trapped – you think he had any sugar?'

'Nope. Didn't see none, or I would've got it for you. Had some polish. I made him a drink out of it to get him drunk – but he spat it out.' Something cried a little inside Guppy. 'Didn't leave a drop. Threw the rest away. Bad waste.'

The fire crackled and hissed, spurting out a blue-green flame. The wood that they had on it wasn't good burning timber. It was some kind of dark stuff that they'd found in a nearby church. It had been carved into images of men and women. Guppy saw a pair of legs peeling and flame licking round them. They didn't give out a lot of heat. Not good burning wood at all.

'Wish we had some books – for the fire,' he said. 'They go best, once the fire's been started some time.'

He poked the ashes with a sliver, trying to get some oxygen underneath the elaborate carvings. As he was doing so, two figures went wandering by in the gloaming of the street. They glanced in, briefly, but carried on when Trader stood up. Guppy was sure that one, or even both, had been women. Sometimes women let you snuggle up close and warm to them at night and it felt good in your belly. You didn't necessarily have to do anything with them – some of them didn't want you to – but it meant you kept each other cosy.

Trader had scared them off though. He looked a violent man: a man full of strength and fury. Guppy knew that underneath Trader was compassionate and kind and one of the last people to get angry to the point of blows.

As the evening advanced, Guppy tried not to think about what was happening to Rupert. There was quite a bit of noise going on around the area, since this seemed to be a heavily populated zone. There was some comfort in that noise. It meant that people were not afraid of giving away their location. Of course, no one would come running to your assistance, if you got into trouble, but it still felt comforting to be amongst a crowd, with voices and domestic sounds to fill the silence.

Where the hell was Rupert?

'We need some more wood,' said Trader.

'Well, I ain't goin' out there to get it. It's too dark. I don't know this district. We'll make do with what we've got . . .'

Guppy stopped short, because of a terrible shriek that seemed to originate in the lungs of the earth and came trumpeting from the subway entrance. Trader jumped about a foot in the air. Guppy's heart hit his lower jaw.

The screaming wail came again, louder and nearer.

Guppy sprang to his feet.

'Jesus!'

The shrieks turned to howls and the person behind them became recognisable. Rupert walked out of the shadows, yelling and laughing intermittently.

'Fooled you that time,' he choked. 'Ha. Ain't nothin' down there but rats and rubbish. No colonies of people with white suits on, all screwin' each other an' having a good time . . .'

'I didn't say they were copulating,' said Trader, huffily.

'Ain't doing that either. Smells like don't-know-what. Probably full of corpses who went in hopin' to start a new civilisation.' Rupert rubbed it in, hard, for the next five minutes. Finally, he produced a mug with a missing handle.

'Found this,' he said.

'Well, that looks nice,' said Trader, glad to be off the hook. 'We could trade that for some sugar.'

Rupert was magnanimous in victory. 'If we meet anybody that happens to have a sackful of sugar and wants a good drinkin' cup, I'll be happy to let you do it, Trader. Until then, we'll use it ourselves.' He held it up to the light of the fire. 'Somethin', eh?'

'Very fine,' said Trader.

Guppy looked at the object with some envy in his breast. He didn't mind that Rupert had found it, but he wished it had been him. Even shoe polish spirit would taste good out of utensil like that. Cans always seemed to add a metallic taste to the fluid they held, though Guppy didn't mind that after a dozen swallows.

'Could I . . . would you let me use it, just sometimes Rupert? When you're not drinkin' something yourself, that is?'

Rupert, leader-of-men, big-hearted, generous.

'Hell, we'll all use it. Take turns, see. Let's start right now. You get somethin' boiling on there, Trader, and then we'll have us each a drink from this cup. Should make us sleep better.'

That night, after his drink, Guppy set some snares in a nearby alley, hoping to catch a dog. When he checked them the next morning, however, there was only a half-dead black cat caught in one of the wire nooses. He dispatched it with a brick and took it back to the others.

'Cat,' he said, holding the carcass for them to inspect.

Rupert nodded in approval. Trader threw some wood on the fire.

'Let's skin her now,' said Rupert. 'I still got the taste of rabbit in my mouth, from a few days back.'

Guppy slit the stomach fur of the still-warm creature with a sliver of glass, and disemboweled it. Then he cut along the inside of each leg, before stripping the skin from the animal like someone peeling off a tight, rubber glove. Finally, he used

Trader's handmade knife to hack off the head, still attached to the hide.

They cut the meat into joints and cooked the flesh in the embers of the fire. Guppy was given the choice of cuts and took a leg. It tasted stringy, but it satisfied.

'Nice tibby,' said Rupert, as he chomped at a bone. 'What's the best grub you've ever had?'

It was their favourite subject. Trader looked thoughtful, before telling the others, 'The best? Dog food, I guess. Most of what I got in these cans is dog food.'

Guppy nodded, enthusiastically.

'Yeah, I like dog too. I once catched this big one. He had yellow . . .'

Rupert laughed.

'Naw, Trader means canned dog food.'

A confusion arose in Guppy's brain.

'You mean they put dog meat in cans?'

More guffaws from Rupert. He looked at Trader and the big man shrugged.

'Don't mock him, Rupert, he can't remember.'

Rupert laughed in spite of this.

'Aw, Gup. It's *pet* food, what Trader's talking about. Rich, gravy-soaked meat in beautiful chunks. They used to feed dogs on it, see? Delicious stuff. An' you find it more often than food for people, because they kept stores of it so their pets wouldn't starve. Some of the people would go hungry themselves rather than let their dogs go without food. Crazy.'

Guppy understood what they were talking about now. He shook his head vigorously and wagged a catbone at Rupert.

'It's not crazy, Rupert, to fatten up a dog before you kill it. That's called livestocking. That's good sense. I know some people who did that – fattened up their pets before they ate 'em.'

Rupert's laugh rang in the subway entrance, echoing down the dark tunnels into the earth's gut.

Chapter Eight

Three blind mice
Didn't stand a chance –
Skewered them on rusty wire,
Cooked them on a charcoal fire.

Though he had never had friends like Trader and Rupert before, Guppy had not always been alone. There was a time, in his late teenage years, when he used to run with a gang – three men and two women. Those were the days when you could find booze, if you were lucky. Fine times he had had with those people.

The only one he could really remember, was Mick, the guy who talked funny because he had come from overseas some-where. Mick had been tall and dark, with a thick black beard which he said was full of small creatures. Mick told everyone he had two heads, especially when he was drunk, which was all the time when booze was around. Mick said he was going to get rid of the bad head, the one on his left shoulder, just as soon as he found a sharp enough knife.

'I don't see no other head,' Guppy told him once, but Mick looked angry.

'That's what they all say,' he snarled, 'but I know different. I *know* it's there – I feel it. It don't matter *you* can't see it, boyo.'

So Guppy never said anything about the head after that, because he hated upsetting people. He used to get upset him-self, when Mick would suddenly jump up and begin screaming, slapping away at his collar bone, shouting, 'Shut up! Shut up! You ain't supposed to be there, you fuckin' deformity. I *hate* it.'

Guppy couldn't remember the other people at all – their faces or their names. Only Mick. Both the women slept with Mick, alternately, and rejected the other two men, who would get angry but be too scared to say anything because Mick was clever with his fists and boots. Guppy didn't care *all* that much, but he could understand why there was an unhappy core to the group. They were like a pack of dogs: always snapping and snarling at one another and only staying together because it was safer to do so. In those days there were gangs that waited for loners and killed and ate anyone slow on their feet.

One day the five – or was it six? – of them came across an old man with a gun, trying to protect a cache of canned food. One of the women talked to the old man, from down in the street, while Mick climbed a rusty fire escape, got in behind him and overpowered him. They stole his gun and his food.

The weapon was an old shotgun with a pitted barrel and only one cartridge.

'One shell – what use is that to a man?' said Mick. 'I ask you, boyo. What use?'

Guppy said he didn't know.

Mick brooded about the fact that they had a weapon but it was only good for one go, until finally he said, 'I've got it. We'll use that shell to get rid of my spare head. You can blow it off my shoulder, Guppy.'

Guppy didn't like the sound of that and began to quake. His experience of guns was limited but he knew they made a noise like the world exploding and he wanted nothing to do with the scheme. Unfortunately he couldn't tell Mick that.

'Wha – what do you want me to do?' he asked.

Mick held the gun by the end of the barrel, the muzzle against the top of his shoulder.

'Get round there,' he said, 'and pull the trigger when I tell you.'

The others vacated the area rapidly, going down to the end of the street and watching from there. Guppy envied them.

'Can't she do it?' he pleaded with Mick, pointing at one of the women. 'She's got good strong hands. Look, mine shake too much . . .' He held out his palms and exaggerated the trembling.

'I don't trust her,' Mick replied. 'She's gettin' jealous of the other one. She might just blow off my good head and call it a mistake. No, I want you to do it Guppy, see. You're the man for the job. I appreciate this, boyo, I really do. You're the surgeon see, about to perform an operation? Get rid of this malignant

61

bastard – it keeps me awake at night, with its jabbering mouth. I hate it, see?'

'I know,' said Guppy, miserably. 'I heard that you hated it.'

'It's a terrible, oversized wart, so it is. Look at it now,' there was a sneer on Mick's face, 'pleadin' for its bloody life. Blow it to bits, Guppy.'

Guppy took hold of the stock and put his finger on the trigger. He closed his eyes, tightly.

'NOW!' screamed Mick.

Guppy pulled the trigger and someone punched him hard in the shoulder throwing him off his feet. At the same time, his head rang like a giant bell. It was a while before he got back on his feet again, sniffing the burning smell in the air.

Mick was on his knees, the others crowded around him. He had his brute hand upon his own shoulder and Guppy could see blood seeping through the thick fingers. His face was very white.

'I'm sorry I hurt you,' cried Guppy. 'Mick? I'm sorry.'

Mick lifted his eyes until they met those of Guppy and there was a white fury within them.

'You stupid bastard,' he hissed, 'you missed. You missed the fuckin' head. It's still there . . .' he lifted his fingers to reveal a raw wound where the shot had taken away a quarter of an inch of shoulder. 'How could you miss, at such close range?'

Guppy turned on his heels and ran, and fortunately Mick was too shocked to follow him.

Months later, when Guppy was rooting through a rubbish dump, the gang came across him again. To his relief and surprise, Mick greeted him like a long lost warrior and slapped him on the back.

'Hey, Guppy boy. Long time no see.'

Apparently the incident with the gun had been forgotten though Guppy noticed that Mick's left arm was rather stiff when he used it.

Guppy stayed with them a couple of days and only when Mick suddenly turned and looked down at his right shoulder and said, 'Ha, thought I didn't notice you moving, eh, damn you . . .' did he sneak away again, to go deeper into the heart of the city, away from his old stamping grounds.

Someone told him later that year that Mick and the gang had gone on a long trek northwards. He had just remembered that when Rupert had been talking about fattening up dogs, because that was just what Mick was planning to do. Mick had gone northwards where there were supposed to be fewer people and more dog packs, in order to start catching them and fattening them up to swop for booze.

Chapter Nine

Jack Sprat would eat no rat,
His wife would eat no mutt.
They left this world in three weeks flat,
Travelling on an empty gut.

One evening, after a long weary day, the three companions came to a huge jungled park which had spread itself beyond its original boundaries and was gradually eating its way into the city. Ragged weeds grew from the derelict ruins around it, and trees had sprung up from the middle of streets and were growing tall and strong, reaching for patches of sky.

They intended to rest at this point, except that the air was full of a strange sound which drew them on, deeper than they might have gone into the old park.

It was music.

'You hear that?' said Rupert, licking his gums. Guppy could see that they were bleeding again.

'I hear it,' said Trader, 'but I don't want to get too close.'

It wasn't that the music was eerie, or weird, or anything like that. On the contrary, it was lively, full of bounce and colour. It danced on the air as if it intended to get every living thing up on its toes and hopping around without a care in the world.

Guppy knew what Trader meant though. It was a worrying sound precisely because it did something with your feelings. It made you want to shout that everything was all right once more: that the world had stepped back into its old ways. Guppy knew that just wasn't true. The music was lying, unless the three men had been living in an area cut off from the real world, and that would be too painful to accept after all these years: to think that everyone else had been having a great time, prosperous, happy, without ill-health.

'That's because we've been talking about the government,' said Trader. 'They're letting us know they're there.'

Throughout the day, he and Rupert had been arguing about where the 'government' had gone. Most of the talk was above Guppy's head, but he gathered that Trader thought the government was still around, watching everybody's move, making sure there was no revolution.

'How can they watch us?' Rupert had said. 'They ain't around, otherwise we would've seen 'em.'

'That's the point. They don't have to be. They got these hidden seeing-eyes that watch us from nooks and crannies. They're sitting around somewhere, looking through these seeing–eyes, right now, listening to every subversive word you've been saying. Soon as they want to make their move, they will. They'll send in men with sticks, to beat the hell out of us, and drag us away somewhere for torture. They've got all sorts of torture machines. Some of them are worked by trained rats. I read that in a book.'

Rupert, Guppy knew, hated it when Trader used his secret world of books – a world from which the other two were locked out – to support his arguments.

'Jesus, that's a tale. You just want to think that so's you can think there's some sort of control out there – somebody lookin' after it all. It's just a mess, Trader. There ain't no govermint left – not even a bad one. A bad one what told everybody what to do all the time, an' no arguments, would be better than this – so you think.'

'We got our freedom,' said Guppy, hoping to get in on this great intellectual debate.

Rupert stared at him in a display of disbelief.

'Freedom to do *what*? To starve? To pick at your sores? Look, a govermint's like a machine. It can work nice and smooth, and everybody's happy, or it can rattle and wheeze away, workin' badly – but as soon as it stops, you ain't got nothing, because the wheels ain't moving any more. You see what I mean?'

'Seems to me,' replied Guppy, 'that if everyone looked after each other, we wouldn't need any government.'

Trader came back in. 'You both got it all wrong. A government is a *family*. The head of the family makes sure everyone has their place. The head of the family can be a bastard, and kick the shit out of you every day, but at least you know where you stand.'

It seemed to Guppy that both Rupert and Trader were saying the same thing, but he said nothing.

Rupert wouldn't leave it alone.

'An' what you're sayin' is that the head of this so-called family is still there,' said Rupert, 'only he or she's hidin' in a cupboard, just watchin' us. The big man is watchin' us, right?'

'You got it. They're looking at us right now.'

'What for?' asked Guppy, innocently.

Trader was a little thrown. Guppy could see it in his face. He rocked back on his heels for a moment.

'Well – to make sure we're doing what we're told.'

'What *for*?'

'Because that's what they want. To be able to feel good, having something we haven't . . .'

'And what's *somethin'*?'

'Power,' said Trader, triumphantly. 'It's what everybody wants.'

Rupert said, 'Crap. The machine ain't goin' nowhere any more. It's stopped. Ain't nobody watchin' us neither. They'd be bored out of their brains within a fuckin' minute. We don't do nothing that's interesting. We just mooch around looking for scraps of grub. Where's the power in that?'

'You think so, but they don't. They know they're manipulating us. They got us where they want us, under their fingers. One guy is out there, head of it all, just moving us around for fun. That's what they do it for, *fun*. They get a good feeling, knowing we're doing just what they want us to do.'

Rupert looked infuriated. He stared around him wildly for a moment and then spotted something amongst some bricks. It was a piece of hard plaster. He picked it up and thrust it into Trader's hands, saying, 'Go and write "govermint" on that wall.'

Trader looked at the thing in his hand and said, 'What?'

'Write *govermint*, damn it. Write it on that wall over there.'

Trader did as he was asked.

Rupert looked at the word suspiciously for a moment.

'You sure that says *govermint*?'

'Sure as I'm standing here.'

Rupert threw open his great coat with a flourish, unhitched his fly, and then proceeded to urinate all over the word until it was obliterated. After the pee, he tucked himself in and shouted at the buildings, 'Take that, you bastards. Sort that one out.'

He then went back to Trader and said, 'You think they manipulated me to do that?'

Trader shook his head gravely. 'One of these days, Rupert, you're going to get yourself into real trouble.'

'I just wished they'd send somebody out here,' replied the little man, 'to knock me around. By hell, I'd have somebody's arse to kick for gettin' us all into this mess then. I hope there was one of those hidden seein'-eyes in that brickwork, because then I would have pissed right into the bastard's face.'

'You do too much swearing,' said Trader, haughtily. 'It doesn't mean anything if you do too much.'

But it was obvious to Guppy that Rupert was pleased with himself. If there was no government, then he had showed Trader the futility of the big man's argument. If there was, then he, Rupert, had just told them where they stood in his estimation.

That morning, Guppy had opened a door in a building and looked into a room. Inside the room, it had been gaily decorated with lots of coloured paper and balloons, and the people inside were wearing funny hats and blowing things out of their mouths. They were all smiling and holding each other, swaying in pairs. There was booze there too, but Guppy knew it wasn't real booze because it came from the wrong side of his brain. So he had to just stand there and watch them guzzle it, knowing that if he went inside, the whole scene would disappear. Everyone was happy. Everyone, except one woman, who was in tears. Someone had his arm around her shoulder.

Guppy wondered whether this had been the government, but he didn't want to mention it to the others because they would want to go back and look. Guppy knew that once the door was opened again, there would be nothing behind it but a dirty old room with trash in the corners and rotten floorboards. So he kept it to himself. Instead, he just listened to the music.

The sounds came from deep inside the parkland where the water would be, so they knew they had to go in and find out who the music-makers were.

As they found their way through the thickets, they came to an area where the grass was short. They looked across this flatland to the lake and were amazed by the sight they saw. There were reflections of lights on the water, from lanterns hanging in the trees, giving the night a festive air. On the shores of the lake were wagons and fires around which people were sitting or standing. There were a lot of high-pitched squeals coming from the children, and chatter from the adults. Nearby, horses were grazing on the lush grass.

If it had not been obvious to Guppy that Trader and Rupert could see these things too, Guppy might have ignored it, thinking it to be one of those scenes that came from the wrong side.

Guppy had never seen a live horse though he had seen pictures once. They looked bigger than he imagined they would be and frightened him by their sheer bulk. He could not remember whether they were savage or not. They *looked* docile, but that was in the light of the lamps. He would reserve judgement.

The music was coming from a woman in long flowing skirts who was standing by the largest fire and playing something with her mouth.

'Harmonica,' said Trader, 'that's what it is.'

'Sure sounds zippy,' said Guppy, with a sigh.

'Makes your balls tingle,' said Rupert, never wanting when it came to expressing himself.

The three of them stood there for a long time, watching this fantasia. It seemed so unreal that it might vanish at any second. These people, in their scarlets and blacks, were actually having a good time. Surely these were the rich people that had abandoned them? They looked kind of self-contained, as if they had never been responsible to anyone for anything.

There was the smell of cooked food in the air which made Guppy's saliva ducts gush with fluid. He dribbled into his beard. Torrents of enzyme were swirling around his stomach. And the music made him feel lightheaded.

Suddenly, someone stepped out of the darkness of the trees. It was a man with a weapon in his hand: a long knife. He approached the three of them as if he had something to protect.

'What do you want?' he asked, when he was about ten yards away.

'Just lookin',' said Rupert, 'what's it to you?' Then he added, 'We never seen you people before. Heard the music.'

Trader added, 'We need some water.'

'We don't want any trouble from you people,' said the man.

'No,' answered Trader, 'we don't want any trouble either. We're just heading north. Who are you?'

'Travellers,' replied the man. 'They used to call us gypsies. Look, we can't feed you. If we went and fed you all, there'd be nothing left for ourselves. You want water, come down by the lake, but don't try anything. I'll be watching you.'

Trader held up his suitcase. 'We got our own food. We don't need yours.'

'Okay. You want to come and get the water?'

They shambled forwards, a little humbly, aware that they were outnumbered by a confident force of people that seemed to have everything under control.

They followed the man to the edge of the lake. He took them round the end of the line of wagons, past the horses. Guppy heard Rupert remark, 'Look at the size of them juicy rabbits,' and he hoped the man had not heard. He had visions of Rupert stealing one of those animals to roast on a spit. By God, it would feed you for half a year!

As Trader and Guppy filled the containers, Rupert stood beside the stranger and asked him how long he had been a 'traveller'.

'We've always been travellers – since the beginning. You've heard of gypsies?'

'No,' said Rupert. 'I never heard of that.'

The man did not offer any more conversation. He just stood with the knife in his hand and watched the three of them closely.

'I don't suppose,' said Rupert, 'we could use one of your fires?'

Suddenly, Guppy was aware that there were others close behind them. He did not look up in case they mistook his action for a hostile move and finished him there and then. He stared into the lake, with its dancing lights, and waited for someone to speak.

A new voice said, 'You can make your own fire, can't you?'

'We can make our own fire,' confirmed Rupert, 'but it would be nice to have a brand. Save us trouble.'

The man with the knife spoke next.

'You can take a brand. I'll bring it to you. Where are you camped?'

'Nowhere yet,' said Rupert, 'but we'll go back to the trees. We won't bother you, closer than that. We'd just like to hear the music for a bit. Leastways, I would. Yours is the only music I've heard for a long time. People don't seem to do that no more. You got to be half-happy to make music.'

A deep, resonant voice quite close to Guppy replied to this.

'That's all right.'

Guppy turned now, very slowly, and in the light of a lamp held by one of his companions, stood an old white-haired man. He had a swarthy complexion and leathery wrinkles, deeply set into his face. They were not the lines of pain or anguish: they seemed to have been placed there on purpose. They suited him. His features would have been wrong without them.

Bright blue eyes appraised Guppy from head to toe. He felt uncomfortable under the old man's gaze, though there was a lot of warmth in it. Guppy could feel it from where he stood. He was aware that his own mouth was open and he shut it, slowly. The old man smiled at him, his face creasing even more. Guppy wanted to walk up to him and hug him, like a child hugs his father, and get some of that warmth for himself.

'Are you God?' asked Guppy. He hadn't meant to say those words. They came from somewhere deep inside him. He couldn't help them creeping into his mouth and making themselves into sounds. Still, he couldn't argue with them.

The old man laughed, and others laughed with him.

'God? I don't think so.'

'He ain't God,' said Rupert, contemptuously. 'He's just an old man.'

The old man chuckled again.

'He's right. Listen to your friend. I wouldn't want to be this God you need so badly. Too much responsibility. Listen, you want to camp right next to us, you can – but you try to steal anything – anything at all – we cut off your

70

hands. You understand? We're not violent people, but we've got to look after our own. That *is* my responsibility. There are too many of you street people out there for us to look after. When the world was working your way, you spurned us, gave us a bad time. Now it's all tipped back in our favour and we don't owe you a thing, you understand? You called us thieves and wasters. We were your scapegoats for a thousand crimes. Well, the boot's on the other foot. I'm telling you this so you understand. We don't mean you any harm – but we don't owe you anything – nothing at all – so it won't prick our conscience if we have to punish you for breaking our laws.'

Trader spoke next.

'We understand, only you got us wrong. We never did anything to you people, even in the old days. We had the same problems ourselves.'

'I'm talking about your kind of people.'

Trader stepped into the light. His mouth had firm lines and his eyes bore down on the old man.

'My people suffered just as much as yours. And these guys – they're just ordinary men.'

'That may be true, but we can't afford to trust you – or anyone. I've told you how we feel. You can camp here if you wish to, but one of my people will stay near you.'

Rupert said, 'That's fine by us, old fellah.'

Guppy thought the old man was wonderful. He still wasn't absolutely convinced that he wasn't God. He sounded just like Guppy expected such a being to sound. His voice had a rich timbre, deep and brown. There wasn't a sharp corner or phlegmy surface to it anywhere. It came out as the voice of God should come out, full and round. He was not a big man, by any means, but it seemed that it would take a horde of Guppys to overwhelm him. He looked so spiritually strong, he had no need of physical strength.

'Thank you, sir,' said Guppy.

'Stop bein' a crawler, Guppy,' said Rupert. 'I'm shamed !'

But the old man just smiled.

'Shouldn't ever call another man that,' he said kindly, 'except you exchange it out of courtesy. No man is better than you.'

With that, the old man and his troupe left them. Only the man with the knife stayed. Rupert went off to gather firewood, and Guppy knew his friend was angry with him. Trader slapped him on the back, though. He understood. Despite Rupert's disapproval, Guppy felt cosy inside. He watched Trader go up to the man with the knife, and heard him say, 'You got any sugar . . .?'

Chapter Ten

There was an old woman
With only one shoe –
The other one went
To making a stew.

It seemed like they were in an island of light on a dark continent. The lanterns hung from the trees like brilliant bee hives, and the fires kept the city outside their range of vision. Gypsy music played for several hours after they had settled, and later, the woman who had played the harmonica came and talked to them.

She was lean and dark, like the old man, with her black hair pulled tightly back from her forehead, pulling her eyebrows into high arches. She had a sharp edge to her voice, but it was not unpleasant, as she sat with her knees tucked up to her chin and her arms wrapped around her shins. They let her sip out of Rupert's good drinking cup.

'You're the shy one,' she nodded at Guppy. 'I can tell.'

Guppy felt himself blushing, furiously.

'I – I – I dunno,' he blurted.

She laughed. 'Yes. I can tell. And you,' she stared at Rupert, 'you're the cocky one.' She looked directly at his groin. 'I can tell that, too.'

Rupert laughed. 'She's a hussy, this one, ain't she though?'

She turned to Trader. 'And you . . .'

'I'm the black one,' said Trader, cutting her short.

'No,' she said, seriously, 'you're the deep one. You got more thoughts in your head than a dozen of these two. What are you going to do with all those thoughts, Mr Deep?'

Trader melted visibly under her charm. Guppy could see his face relax and a soft look came into his eyes.

Trader shrugged, 'Oh, I don't know. They're not very practical thoughts. Not the kind that help you survive, day to day.'

'The world still needs its philosophers.'

'Yeah, I guess so. I hope it does.'

She asked all three, 'Did you like my music?'

Guppy swayed on his bottom.

'I thought it was wonderful. I ain't never heard nothin' like that in my whole life. Where'd you learn such stuff? It was exciting – yet sad, too. It made me want to dance and cry, both at once. I love that music.'

Her eyes opened wide and she smiled.

'My – not so shy after all, and he's stealing a few of your thoughts, Mr Deep.'

Guppy flushed again. He wondered if she were mocking him, but a quick look at her face told him she was not.

She wasn't a young woman by any means, though she had weathered better than a street woman of her age. She seemed to have kept a sparkle which was absent from most people of the streets, with their ailments brought on by damp and cold, lack of nutritious food, attacks from disease and, in the case of women, attacks from brutal males.

She reached out towards Guppy.

She touched his cheek and said, 'When is your birthday?'

Guppy blinked hard. 'I dunno.'

The woman looked around at all of them.

'Do any of you know when your birthdays were?'

A shaking of heads.

'Never mind, I'll have to guess by your eyes. I can do that.'
She turned back to Guppy.

It seemed a bit spooky, and he didn't like the way the other two were looking at him.

'Guppy, isn't it? Yes. Well, Guppy, you're a Gemini . . .'

'I am?' He was surprised. The way she said it made him sound special. He had always felt very ordinary. He wondered where in his eyes it said that he was a Gemini.

'A Gemini. Let others now see you at your most determined and self-assured. Difficult times are ahead, but you must not retreat into your shell. The period is fast approaching when you simply have to finalise certain long-term plans or make a decisive move. The approaching new moon can create friction and even a parting of the ways if you let it. You should triumph over your adversaries . . .' She peered closer, as if surprised. 'One man in particular needs to fear you – a man with power, who believes himself safe.'

Guppy was desperately impressed. Although he understood very little of what she told him, he could feel the truth of her words in his breast. It seemed he was quite an important person, if all those things were going to happen to him. And he just thought he was *ordinary* – Trader had called him ordinary. It just showed you. Yes sir, it just showed you.

It was Rupert's turn next. He was told he had entered one of the most decisive periods of the year for professional matters, and he must forget about being liked or admired, and make it clear what he expected, above all, what he would no longer tolerate or accept.

'So many powerful aspects now relate to your security. You must be wondering when the next blow is going to be delivered, but this is really the final stage in a long, drawn-out period of conflict, setbacks and disappointments.'

Trader did not want her to prophesy him at first, but eventually he relented, after lots of verbal stroking from the gypsy woman.

'If you feel overcommitted then this is the perfect time to divest yourself of certain responsibilities, but above all take partners and close associates into your confidence, and appreciate just how much more can be accomplished through joint undertakings and endeavours. Be prepared for an unusual amount of opposition if you do forge ahead with important changes or plans, but others have had fair warning of your intentions.'

Trader nodded seriously.

'They sure have. Is there anything about sugar? Will I find any sugar?'

'Could be. There's something fuzzy there, I can't quite make out. Perhaps you won't need the sugar?'

Trader looked happy.

'Just so long as something's coming, that's all that matters.'

She went away from them after that, and back to her own people, but later in the night Guppy saw her return. She slipped under Rupert's coat and after a while there were some furtive sounds and a lot of breathing going on. Then she went away again.

An hour later, she was back, this time to crawl in beside Trader. Guppy heard Trader say, 'Eh? What?' in surprise, and the gypsy shushed him, softly, murmuring into his ear. A few minutes later Trader began grunting, in a muffled way, as if he were trying to keep his voice down but was having great difficulty. Guppy was glad that Rupert was fast asleep. He wondered how the little man would feel if he knew that his most recent conquest had gone from his bed to that of another, within an hour.

The gypsy left.

Soon, Guppy could hear the snores of Trader joining with those of Rupert. There was a sound from the darkness. She was back again. She slipped down beside Guppy and he felt her warm hands on him. He didn't say anything. He just found his own hands inside her little jacket and needles began pricking him all over his body. It was so good he wanted to stay with her all night – forever – but shortly after he had finished, she left him. That was sad, but he still felt as if he had a fire in his belly. It kept him warm for the rest of the night.

The following morning both Rupert and Trader carried smiles in the corners of their mouths. When the gypsy came to visit them there was a lot of shuffling of feet and sidelong glances going on. She gave each one of them equal attention and asked if they were staying for another night.

'Hell, we ain't in any hurry, are we?' said Rupert, much too quickly.

Trader agreed with a solemn shake of the head. They both looked at Guppy but he didn't know what to say or do, so eventually Rupert said, 'Well, that's settled then. We stay on another night – so long as you people don't mind, that is.'

'We don't own the park,' she replied.

The day was pretty lively, with children and lean fast dogs running all over the place. Guppy eyed the latter with surprise, since they didn't have a spare ounce of meat on them and would barely have made a decent soup, let alone a stew. Guppy wondered why the gypsies bothered to keep the animals at all.

The woman took Guppy to see the horses when she noticed his fascination with the creatures. Confronted by them, he was afraid to go close and stroke their noses the way she did. They were enormous animals. It seemed they only ate grass, but Guppy didn't trust them just the same.

Later, she talked about her travels. She told the three men that the gypsies moved from park to park, and that there were other bands of travellers who did the same.

Rupert asked, 'You ever been out of the city?'

'Never. We don't need to. Long ago we used to have to stick to rail sidings and wasteland areas, but the parks are open to us now – most of them. We can do more or less what we like.'

The old man came to their fire and talked with them a little. He seemed to have taken to Guppy and praised him as an upright man. Guppy felt ten feet tall. When the pair had gone, Trader said they should have mentioned the fact that they were on their way to the airport, to see if there was a space ship there which would take them to the stars, but Rupert was against this.

'We can't get all these people an' dogs an' horses in a small space ship. They wouldn't fit. Maybe – maybe we got room for the lady? What do you think?'

'Could be,' said Trader, non-committally, 'but she might not come with us.'

'I think she would,' said Rupert. 'I think she kinda likes us – 'specially old Guppy here. She's got a soft spot for him all right. You can see it.'

Guppy just kept thinking to himself about what she had said to him, when they had done it last night. She had kept whispering in his ear, 'Last is best – last is best,' the words getting quicker and quicker all the time, until the final, ' . . . beeeest,' had slid out, in a long, snaky sigh.

That night, all three men stayed awake until well into the small hours, each taking sneaky looks at the gypsy camp, expecting a figure to come drifting towards their fire. She never came and eventually sleep overtook each hopeful form, until all three were dead to the world.

When the sun woke them, they were devastated to find that the gypsies had broken camp and left nothing behind them but marks on the ground. They stared at the empty spot in bewilderment, half expecting her to appear from some place in the bushes, if only to say goodbye.

Of course, she never came, and eventually they made their own preparations for leaving, in disappointed silence. Guppy felt very heavy inside. He hadn't felt so leaden for months. He only hoped she felt as sad as he did, and kept some warm thoughts of him in her head.

Rupert became very irritable.

'Okay, we goin' or what? I ain't hanging around here all day waiting for the end of the world. Let's get this thing moving. We gotta be on the road. Guppy for chrissakes, will you move your arse? Trader, what the hell are you . . .' and so on, like that, for the rest of the morning, even when they were out of the park and walking.

Guppy understood. He felt a little of it himself, but he kept it bottled up inside, nice and tight. If two of them let it out, the way Rupert was doing, there would be one hell of a fight and they might all split up, regretting it later.

The endless streets stretched before them. They were back amongst the abandonati once more, coming across groups of people that looked only half human beside the gypsies. How could one section of the population survive so well, while the other was in such dire straits? It didn't seem fair. But then, thought Guppy, when was anything ever fair? Things had always been like this – one lot being better off than the rest. You just had to scratch at your fleas and sores, and suffer the indignities of weak bowels and live with it.

One thing he could be thankful for: he had two good companions. Whenever he stopped to count his blessings on his fingers, he at least reached the second digit.

The night came down in a hail of frozen rain, out of season. They sought shelter from the storm and found it in an attic where the sound hammered around them. The noise of the hail on the loose slates was aggressive, as if it were trying to beat the world to its knees.

'Fuckin' weather,' snarled Rupert.

Guppy knew his friend was wishing that the storm was in human shape, then he could go outside and beat the shit out of it, to get rid of his frustrations. *Isms*, Trader called them.

Rupert was full of isms, like little demons, that needed letting out every so often.

They had a long and lonely night, full of wishes. Bones creaked restlessly in aching joints; throats produced harsh, ominous coughs; bellies rumbled noisily. Unable to sleep, Guppy thought about what the gypsy had told him, that somewhere a powerful man went in fear of him. That was difficult to believe, since Guppy would not knowingly hurt anyone. Besides, how could he, a street person, do anything to anyone in a position of power? It didn't make sense. *Did it?*

Chapter Eleven

Tom, Tom, the piper's son
Stole longpig and away he run.

There comes a time in any epic journey when the travellers grow weary and dispirited and begin quarrelling amongst themselves. A time when there is a danger of the whole enterprise crumbling and falling away. For the trio, that crisis was reached the day after they left the gypsies. All three men were depressed by the fact that there was another kind of life available, but not to them. They felt cheated and confused. They began to resent each other, thinking that, had they been alone, they might have charmed the gypsies into taking one more on board.

They forgot, quite conveniently, that they would never have met the gypsies if they had remained alone. Guppy's mind dwelt on warm nights and music, and he knew the other two had similar preoccupations. He resented sharing these daydreams with anyone, even Trader and Rupert. *Especially* Trader and Rupert. He became possessive of the memory of the gypsy woman and grew angry inside when he saw a smile around the mouth of Rupert, or a wistful look on the face of Trader. These two men were encroaching on his own fantasy.

'What are you smiling at?' he snapped at Rupert.

Rupert raised his eyebrows. 'Mind your own goddamn business.'

Yet he felt it was his business. It was more his business than Rupert's, and the runt had no right to be thinking those thoughts which belonged to Guppy. Rupert was stealing the very pictures out of his head and using them for himself. How the gypsy could have got into bed with Rupert, or Trader for that matter, Guppy had no idea. One was a great clumsy oaf and the other a skinny little rat. Surely she had only done it to be polite to the other two. *Last is best*, he reminded himself. *Last is best*. Poor Trader – poor Rupert – he should feel sorry for them really. They had been too busy sleeping, before and after their sexual experiences, to know the whole truth. Only Guppy knew that.

They passed along a street where pretty young boys hung out of windows and called to them softly, to come up and see them. Rupert threw stones at the little cherubs, with their dark locks falling over pale faces, and their big eyes round with innocence, appealing to passers-by. Their sweet faces ducked as the small man lobbed half bricks at them with alarming accuracy.

'There's no need for that,' said Guppy, hotly.

Rupert the wise man, nodded sagely.

'You think. You *think*. I *know* what those little bastards are up to – used to do it myself, one time. You go through those doors and they'll castrate you and leave you without a stitch.'

'I don't believe you,' said Guppy. 'I 'specially don't believe you ever looked like one of them. You couldn't have – a runt like you.'

'You watch your mouth.'

'Yeah? You gonna shut it for me? I ain't scared of you, pal. I still know how to handle myself.'

'Okay – okay – you like little boys? Go up and get your balls cut off. See if I give a damn. You don't use 'em anyway.'

'That's what you think, you puffed-up little squirt. You was asleep. Anyways, I don't like boys. I'm a ladies' man.'

Trader had stopped walking and was looking at both men with a worried expression on his face. His eyes flicked from one aggressive man to the other. Rupert now confronted Guppy, invading his personal space and pushing his sharp nose right up to the other man's jaw.

His voice was thunderous.

'Whaddya mean? I was asleep?'

Guppy snarled at the nose.

'You – you snored all through it. After she was with you, she went to Trader, an' then after that, to me. Last is best, she said. She said so, see. She was just trying you out, to see if you matched up. Seems you didn't.'

'FUCK YOU!' roared Rupert.

Guppy smiled maliciously. 'Yeah, she did, didn't she?'

A glance at Trader told Guppy volumes. He looked like someone who had been informed by a good friend that his wife actually hated him and only stayed for the sake of the children. Guppy began to retreat a little.

'How come . . . ?' began Trader.

Guppy did not know what he was going to say, but answered anyway.

'Dunno,' he said darkly.

Rupert, who it now seemed had not believed Guppy when he said it the first time, stared at Trader and had his confidence shattered for him by the black man's expression. Clearly, the gypsy woman had been with Trader too.

'You mean, she really did go with you guys?'

Guppy and Trader nodded miserably.

'Shit!' Now Rupert's dream had been smashed too. He sagged, bending over like a little old man.

'She went with *all* of us,' he said bleakly.

They stared at one another resentfully.

'I've a good mind to leave you guys to screw yourselves up,' said Rupert. 'I've a good mind to march right out of here, an' go my own road.'

'Good riddance,' said Guppy.

'Hope you starve,' said Trader, gripping the case of food tightly.

The little man stood there with his hands thrust deep into his pockets, glaring at the ground. Trader looked around him as if searching for an arbitrator, and Guppy felt an irrational flush of elation in having wounded Rupert.

It might have ended there. They might have all given each other the finger and walked off in different directions had not adversity thrust itself into their path once again, to unite them. While they had been arguing, six men had come round the corner and spread themselves across the street. They were all armed with clubs. They looked hard and mean. Guppy was the first to comment.

'Hey,' he said, 'we got company.'

The other two turned. Trader clutched at his suitcase. Guppy still had enough anger in him to resent the intrusion.

'What are you lookin' at?' he snarled.

One of the men stepped forward. He had a large bullet-shaped head, too large for his body, with a massive nose-breaking brow. His arms were thick and muscled and he thwacked the club he held against the palm of his left hand.

'Gimme the bag,' he said.

Trader took a backward step, Rupert a forward one.

'Or what?' said Rupert.

'You want your fuckin' head broke? Gimme the bag.'

Guppy moved now. He lined himself up with Trader, his legs shaking a little as they prepared themselves for flight. Guppy quite expected to stay and help Rupert fight these men, but his legs had other ideas.

Trader cried, 'Run!' and ducked down a side alley. Guppy's legs followed him. Then Rupert.

They ran the length of the alley, but on reaching the end found their way blocked by a huge natural lake which had formed in the hollow of an underground collapse. A subway station or confluence of sewers had originally been directly below this point, but the road had fallen in and the hole had filled with rainwater. There was a large whirlpool in the centre where the water was draining away along subsurface tunnels. It moved slowly at the edges, gathering speed towards the middle, where it made a sucking sound as it dragged water and debris into its belly. There was no way the three men could cross the maelstrom and live.

'What are we goin' to do, Rupert?' asked Guppy.

'Oh, so it's *Rupert* again, is it? What happened to the *runt*? Where did the *skinny little rat* go?'

'I never called you that last. I said *squirt* – I never said *rat*. I wouldn't call you that, Rupert.'

'Oh, well that makes all the difference, don't it? I should feel better for that.'

Guppy did not answer, but the small man had had his say and was now apparently willing to let bygones fly away on the wind. His brow furrowed in thought as he put his mighty cunning to work on the problem. Presumably the group of men were just waiting at the entrance to the alley, knowing that their prey could not escape.

'Maybe we can buy our way out? C'mon. Let's go back. We ain't going anywhere this way.'

They walked slowly down the length of the alley. Sure enough, when they stepped out into the street, the opposition was waiting for them. Rupert stepped forward.

'Whaddya say to a can of food each, an' then you let us pass, eh? We'll pay the toll, but we gotta keep some for ourselves, ain't we?'

The man with the big head looked back at his friends, then turned to Rupert.

'Come and get some stake pie, runt,' he said.

Rupert muttered, 'That's the second time today somebody called me that. I ain't takin' no more.'

He turned to Trader and asked for the suitcase. Trader was reluctant to give it to him, no doubt thinking Rupert was going to hand it over. But the little man said, 'It's okay,' and pulled it from Trader's grasp.

Rupert untied the case and took out the metal pipe. Then he turned to face big head, twirling the length of pipe in his fingers like a drum majorette's baton. Guppy had to admit that Rupert looked very impressive, if a little showy.

'Just you an' me,' cried Rupert to big head, but even before the words were out of his mouth all six men moved in on him and clubbed him to the ground. He hardly managed to get a swing at their legs before they kicked the pipe out of his hand and stamped on his fingers.

Trader tried to run but they tripped him and snatched the case. Guppy managed to avoid any blows and fled halfway down the street. When he looked back, Trader was on his feet and the men were disappearing round the corner with their provisions. Rupert lay still and Guppy trudged slowly back. He felt guilty because he had run, but his instinct for self-preservation was stronger than any other – it had been developed over many years in the streets and was now uncontrollable – and he knew he would do the same thing again.

Guppy felt drained as he approached Trader who was lifting Rupert onto his shoulders.

'Is he dead?' he asked, fearful of the answer.

Trader said, 'I can still feel him breathing, but he's hurt bad.'

They took him back down the alley, to the edge of the whirlpool, and Trader lay him on the ground. Guppy dipped a rag in the water and wiped Rupert's face with it. After a while the little man opened his eyes. There were two large bruises on his forehead but his hand was pressed to his side.

He coughed a little, then said, 'Bastards got me in the kidneys . . . '

'You ain't got a fractured skull then?' said Guppy, who was more worried about a lump he could see appearing on Rupert's temple.

'Naw, why? Disappointed?'

'Aw, don't be that way, Rupert,' said Guppy, almost in tears. 'I didn't mean nothin' before, you know that.'

Rupert began to nod his head, then thought better of it. He tried to sit up but Trader had to help him, supporting his back against his knee.

'Sure as hell hurts,' said Rupert. He felt his several wounds. 'They didn't bother that much, so long as I went down, an' I went down quick as I could, I can tell you that for nothing. Caught me a few when I fell, but I was going away from the blows – rode 'em see? I still got a few tricks. Hell, as soon as I saw them all comin' in, I knew I'd screwed up . . . ' He rubbed his side. 'Wish they'd leave my damn kidneys alone – hurts when I piss already, without gettin' booted.'

'You got courage, Rupert,' said Trader. 'I admire you for that.'

'Yeah, well, they got the grub. Sorry Trader.'

'All except the two cans I put in my pockets, while you were going at them,' said Trader.

'Yeah? Well, they won't have them for long,' said the little man. He tried to get to his feet but fell over again. They took him, one on each arm, and made their way to a building just near the alley to rest for the night.

For the next twenty-four hours Rupert had a fever and began yelling and screaming, when he wasn't out cold. His face was a pasty grey, and hot and cold sweats took turns to soak his body. Trader nursed him as best he could, which simply meant patting his blankets every so often and giving him as much hot water as he could get down him. Guppy sat in the corner feeling guilty and miserable. Somehow he felt responsible for Rupert's condition, and though he knew that if he had gone to help he would be in the same or perhaps a worse condition, he still couldn't help feeling he should have done something. Friends were supposed to help one another, even to the death. It sounded good and right when you said it afterwards, but when stuff like that was going on all you could think of was to save yourself.

Guppy still did not understand Rupert. Why had he gone to fight the big-headed man? Anyone could see that it was a silly gesture. They should have just handed over the cans and run. That was the sensible thing to do. But Rupert had to show them he wasn't afraid of them for some reason, which was crazy. It was like throwing yourself off a tall building because someone had mocked you for being scared of heights. Didn't make sense at all.

Guppy remembered such behaviour from street gangs he had encountered. He had thought it was crazy even then. It was something to do with proving manhood, but then Guppy had never understood what that word 'manhood' really meant. It seemed to mean that you kicked the guts out of anyone who stood up to you, until somebody managed to kick the guts out of you. So why should he feel guilty for running away? It was stupid. But he did. He felt as guilty as hell, and it made him feel worse when Rupert was thrashing and groaning under his blankets.

The hours were long while they waited for Rupert to recover and the situation was made worse by the fact that they had to eke out their rations. Guppy went on a rat hunt, hoping to revert to his old diet, but he seemed to have lost the knack of flicking them into the air and kicking them against a wall.

At dawn the next day, a group of youngsters, girls and boys, came into the building. They were probably the same group that had called down to the men from the glassless windows. There was a sort of stand-off in the hallway, with Trader towering, hands on hips and looking like a hulk, and Guppy waving the metal pipe, but the gang soon indicated that they wanted no trouble. They said they thought the place was empty, and they left.

Towards evening, that day, Rupert showed signs of getting better. He was sweating less, and sat up, asking for some food. Trader gave him what he could and then the little man went back to sleep, but it looked like a normal rest rather than a feverish one.

The following morning Rupert was up and ready to go before the others had crawled from beneath their blankets.

'Are we goin' on?' said Guppy.

'Course we're going on. What else?'

'But we ain't got no food.'

Rupert's eyes narrowed.

'We're going to get our own stuff back,' he said.

It seemed that manhood still had to be proved, even after being beaten and almost killed.

'How are we going to do that?' asked Trader, looking as daunted as Guppy felt.

Rupert buttoned his huge coat and shuffled it to a comfortable position, as if it were an armour-plated shell, an exoskeleton that would stop blows in the coming confrontation. He tightened the binding round his shoes, then spat on his hands and slicked back his hair and sparse beard. He looked even more like a rat, once that had been done, but he also looked mean. He rolled the sleeves of his greatcoat, up to the elbows. Then he picked up the metal pipe, gave it a few spins, before saying:

'We're goin' to go to plan B.'

'Which is what?' asked Trader.

'We try to sneak the stuff away and beat the shit out of anyone who tries to stop us. I had enough of bein' kicked around. I'm gonna do some kickin' myself . . . '

Chapter Twelve

Jack and Jill went up the hill
To fetch a pail of water.
Jack was killed by packs of dogs
And Jill died shortly after.

Rupert, followed by the other two, retraced their steps to the section of the road where the child-gangs lured men off the streets. He called up to them, asking them to send someone out to talk to him. Eventually four kids stepped out of the building. Their spokesman was a dark-skinned boy of about twelve years.

'What you want? We ain't done nothin' to you.'

Rupert grinned. 'Nah, it's nothin' like that. What it is, see, is we want to know something.'

'What?'

'Where those guys – you must've seen 'em – big men – six of 'em – where they stay around?'

'We don't know no big guys.'

'Hey, yeah you do. One's got a head this size.' Rupert held his hands apart about two feet and the kids grinned and nudged each other. 'You know who I mean. They run some sort of toll – make you pay before you pass – that kinda thing.'

'So what if we know him?' said the dark kid.

Rupert reached into one of his large pockets and came out with his handleless cup.

'I got a good drinking-cup here. It's yours, you tell us where they are.'

He held it up as if it were priceless. Rupert always managed to be impressive, giving the transaction an air of great importance.

There was a whispered conference among the youngsters, then the dark kid said, 'You tell 'em we told you an' we're dead.'

Rupert's gesture was expansive.

'You want the cup or not?'

The kid stepped forward and snatched the object from his hand. Then he walked back to his companions and they strolled towards their building. Guppy thought they were going to steal the cup, without giving them the information – and he was secretly glad – but at the last minute the dark kid turned.

'The place you stayed? It's two blocks further on from there. There's an old wreck just outside the door. I ain't taking you there, so don't ask.'

He disappeared into the building.

The three men went on a foray and found the shell of a truck outside a place which was once, according to Trader, called the 'Rock'. The original sign was gone, but the letters had been weathered into the brickwork above the door. The three men sat in a building opposite and waited for dark. They talked in whispers, about the gypsy woman, this time without recriminations. Already the event formed part of a nostalgic history they were building up around themselves, so that each one in turn could say, 'Hey, remember when . . . ' and recall some incident which the others would enjoy in the retelling.

When night came they rested through the evening and on, until the early hours. While it was still dark, Rupert crept across the road and peered in one of the windows. He said he could not see anything, but was going in.

' . . . you watch the door. If anybody comes out, before me, hit the bastard.'

He handed his metal pipe to Trader, who passed it quickly on to Guppy.

Rupert slipped through the window. Not long after he had entered, there was a sound in the hallway, and shortly afterwards, a man appeared in the doorway.

It was big head.

They could see the enormous shape in silhouette. He stopped in the doorway and looked out down the street. Guppy and Trader were hidden behind the corner and Guppy wondered what to do. Rupert had said to hit anyone who came out, but that was harder than it looked. First you had to get close to them and the man would see him coming.

His shoulders shook violently whenever he thought about going to attack the man, and there was the worry that Rupert was still inside. If only the moon was not so bright! The man would be sure to yell out when he saw Guppy coming. Rupert would be trapped inside.

Big head stepped out a little, into the street.

Trader whispered, 'He knows something is wrong. Where the hell is Rupert?'

The figure before them looked as solid as rock. He sniffed the night air, noisily, as if this would give him clues as to why he had been disturbed. He didn't seem in any hurry to do anything.

A dog wandered out of an alley, saw the man, and trotted away down the street, glancing back occasionally to see if it were being followed. The man stared after the hound and muttered something inaudible to Guppy. Then he kicked at a stone and sent it spinning along the gutter.

Just at that moment a furtive shape appeared in the doorway behind big head and froze there.

It was Rupert, carrying the case of food.

For a while nobody moved. The man still faced the street and Rupert was locked in position, one knee bent in the act of walking. Then big head looked behind him and went, 'Wha . . . ?' Rupert still did not move. Big head spun round to confront him.

Guppy's legs began to move. He was running over the street and almost collided with the man. He swung the pipe at the last second, at big head's back, but his victim must have heard something because he jumped into the air. The pipe caught him behind the knees. There was a sharp cracking sound, the man did a semi-flipflop, and went down heavily on his side. He yelled, loudly.

Rupert dashed forward and, without pausing in his stride, kicked him in the mouth, calling over his shoulder, 'Take that, you scud . . .'

None of the trio spoke. They just kept running north until they found a building which had a lot of exits. They dashed inside, their chests heaving. There was a family in there, sleeping on the floors, and they grumbled as the three men stepped around them. The trio found an empty room and sat in a corner, as close as they could get to one another, and just listened.

After a long while, Rupert said, 'If they come, we just make tracks out back, okay?'

The other two nodded.

Later, when there were no sounds of chase, Trader whispered, 'Is it all there?'

Rupert replied, 'Course it's not all here. The bastards have eaten half of it.' He opened the case and felt around inside. 'There's about twelve, maybe fifteen cans left.'

'They ate more than half,' wailed Trader.

'We're lucky to get this back. Hell, Guppy, you sure gave that bastard a belt. Reckon you busted his leg. Serve the fucker right. I wished I had time to cave in his skull for him, like he tried with me.'

Guppy felt sick and elated, both at the same time. He couldn't get the cracking sound out of his head. It was the first time he had ever hurt anyone, seriously, and he wasn't sure he would rather it had been Trader who had done the hitting. If they ever caught up with him . . . well, it didn't bear thinking about. They would kill him with a thoroughness he could well visualise.

'We're having a real adventure,' said Trader. He sounded strangely satisfied with the situation.

Guppy felt the runs coming on and his sphincter muscle started screaming for action, but he did not dare leave the other two. He held himself in tightly. He hoped he wasn't in for a bout of dysentery. The last one, about a year previously, had almost killed him off. Maybe it was just a touch of diarrhoea. He hoped it was just that.

He slept, fitfully.

By morning his stomach and bowels had stopped gushing around and he felt a little better. He went outside and found an alley. When he got back, the other two were awake.

'We better get on the road,' said Rupert, 'an' put a few blocks between us and those maniacs back there. I think they ain't the sort to follow, though. They're territory animals – know what I mean? They got to stick to their own area or they get scared.'

'Them? Scared? I don't believe that,' said Trader. 'Just because they're tough, don't mean they don't get scared,' said Rupert. 'Look at you – you're a big guy – but you get scared.'

Trader's eyes flashed.

'What do you mean by that?'

'Oh, I don't mean nothin' by it, Trader. You're a passyfist – you told me.' Rupert nodded at Trader and said to Guppy, 'He don't believe in hurtin' people. Well, I don't either – not for nothing. I wouldn't kick a guy just for looking at me, the way some do. But you gotta protect yourself, ain't you? You know what I mean, Guppy. You an' me's of the same mind.'

Guppy replied, 'I sort of agree with both of you.'

'Well,' said Rupert, 'I think you got to make up your mind, one way or the other. Otherwise, when the time comes to face it out, you're too busy trying' to make up your mind whether to stick or run. We got to get ourselves another piece of pipe. I don't mind being the one to protect us, but I got to have your support Guppy, or we ain't gonna make it, see? Trader – I know where he stands. But I got to know about you, one way or the other. I woulda thought after last night, you knew what you was – a passyfist or a nose-buster.'

'I'll think about it,' said Guppy, defiantly.

And they left it at that. Rupert was obviously not satisfied but he didn't push the matter further. It would have been no good anyway, because Guppy was feeling stubborn and he wasn't going to be forced into a decision.

Guppy stared out of the window at the cars sliding down the street. They sparkled with raindrops in the morning light and their windshields glistened as if formed from tiny fragments of crystal. A yellow one went by, looking solid and sturdy amongst the fancy colours of the other vehicles. The driver of this car had a cap on, which Guppy envied very much. It had a peak – a shiny black peak – which jutted aggressively from the cloth part. Guppy felt that if he had a hat like that, he would not need to be a nose-buster. A cap like that would scare everyone away without him having to do anything at all.

'Jesus, Guppy, you listenin' to what I say?' broke in Rupert's voice. 'You're allus dreaming, with that stupid look on your face. What are you thinkin' of, for chrissakes?'

'Nothin',' said Guppy. 'I just get lost in my head sometimes.'

'Find your way out of the damn thing, we got to get going,' said the exasperated Rupert. 'The way you talk about your head, anyone would think you could walk around inside it.'

The long trek continued, through the cluttered and occasionally peopled streets, until they came to an area which was full of old warehouses and broken cranes, some of which were lying stretched on the ground like the skeletons they had seen in the museum. It was a sad sight for some reason and brought a lump to Guppy's throat. It was like a graveyard for extinct animals, where the wind blew through rusty metal bones and empty tombs.

Rupert said it gave him the creeps, but Trader seemed to like it.

'This is it,' said the black man.

'This is what?' asked Rupert.

'The last place I saw my mom. Yeah, we got off the boat not far from here, I'm sure of it. And I wandered around this place for days, looking for her, when she disappeared. Maybe she's still around here, somewhere?'

Rupert put a hand on his friend's arm.

'Trader – that was years ago. She'd be dead by now. Anyway, there must be dozens of places like this. How do you know you've got the right one?'

'I remember these cranes.'

He walked forward, inspecting a fallen giant. Rupert looked at Guppy and shrugged.

Guppy said, 'Rupert's right, Trader. This could be anywhere – they's lots of cranes all over. I seen 'em before, too.'

'But I don't *want* it to be anywhere. I want it to be the place.'

'It ain't a matter of what you want, it's a matter of . . . well, if it's *right*. You can't just make a place into somewhere you want it to be,' said Rupert, 'can you?'

Trader glanced behind him.

'Why not? It doesn't matter, does it? If they all look alike and you can't tell one from the other, this is just as good a place as any. I want to stay around here for a while.'

Rupert rolled his eyes.

'We can do it. We can do it. But I don't see how it'll help any. I wish I could find my pa, too, but I know I can't. He's dead. We all got to go sometime.'

Trader nodded. 'I never saw my mother die. To me she's still around, somewhere, and this is as good a place as any, like I said. Don't worry, I'm not going to go out looking for her. I'd just like to think that she's somewhere nearby, while I stay here. Okay?'

He stood there with the wind blowing through his white beard, looking like a man who has come home. Guppy felt awkward, as though he were intruding on some private family gathering, a reunion. It wasn't that he believed he was unwelcome, but he couldn't see the same things that Trader saw. There were no memory-pictures to help him feel an affinity with his surroundings. Good memories, bad memories, it didn't matter. He hadn't got either. He just felt like a stranger in Trader's land. Nevertheless, he said to Rupert, 'Let's stay here for a bit. We can stay, can't we, and let Trader rest a bit?'

'We can stay. We can stay.'

It was not an ideal environment, Guppy knew that. The wind was sharp and cold, with little to thwart it. It came careering around the corners, looking for someone to blow through, someone's teeth to set clacking. Still, if it would help Trader, why not stay?

They camped for the night in the corner of a warehouse. There was nothing in there but space. All sounds they made were thrown back at them by the vastness of the building and it gave the place a spooky atmosphere, as if at any moment they might hear someone laughing softly in the steel rafters above their heads. Even Trader admitted that much.

The wind rattled the corrugated steel walls and lifted the roof occasionally in one corner, letting it go down with a bang. Outside, there was flapping sheet metal on the adjacent building, sounding like some great metal bird trying to take to the air with wounded wings.

From the centre of the warehouse roof hung a huge hook from thick chains. The hook was almost the same height as Guppy and it looked to be beckoning him every time his eyes caught the object. He didn't like that. It added to the ghostliness of the place. It was impossible to sleep there, what with all the noise and that hook, and Guppy was later sorry that he had agreed with Trader.

He wondered whether to go outside and find somewhere more comfortable to sleep, but he was scared of those cranes. At any moment another giant metal insect might come crashing down, and even if it didn't hit him, it would scare the hell out of him.

In the middle of the night he heard something metal rolling past the warehouse. He went outside to have a look. It was an empty oil drum, holed by rust, which the wind was pushing backwards and forwards. Guppy watched this object for a while as it was sent on its short voyages from nowhere to nowhere. Then with his eyes on the cranes, he went warily through the yards on a walk to the sea.

He could smell the ocean on the wind and though he had never seen it before, he knew what it was. At the end of the dockyard were piles of round objects, with markings, built into pyramid shapes. Beyond these was the harbour wall.

He stood on the wall and looked out, over the moonlit waters of the harbour, to the wine dark sea. It was a fascinating sight. *No buildings.* No buildings at all. Just a flat stretch of nothing but water and sky. Out on the horizon were short strips of lights, five in all, one above the other. They were moving slowly through the night.

'People out there,' he said to himself. 'They must be pretty scared . . . '

He watched as the lights disappeared, down a hole on the other side of the world, and then went back to bed. This time, he slept.

Chapter Thirteen

Good meat is brown, dilly dilly,
Bad meat is green.
I didn't care, dilly dilly –
Poisoned my spleen.

Two army officers sat in their cramped cell in the overcrowded bunker three hundred feet below the ground. They were drinking heavily and leaning against the wall for support.

'Well, Colonel,' said the short one with the moustache, 'when do you think it'll be safe to go up?'

'Oh, my guess is two more years. Is there any more of that booze left in the bottle?'

'Sure – say, it'll be nice to see the sky again. We've waited a long time. Who do you think won? – the war I mean.'

The colonel shrugged.

'Them – us – who cares? We gave as good as we got, that's all that counts. Sure we lost a few cities, and the rest of them are probably falling to pieces by now, but what the hell, that's what war's all about. You can't have a battle without knocking a few bricks down.

'They'll be some clearing up to do – the first thing is to get organised and bring that rabble up there under some sort of control. I expect they're eating each other by now. Goddamn savages the human race, given a chance. Take away authority, discipline, and it all falls to pieces. The proof's up there now . . .'

The major nodded.

'You mean, we have to get them building again – start industry going, that sort of thing?'

'Well, yes – eventually – but the first thing to do is pull everything together and crush any resistance. Knock a bit of respect back into those savages up there. Don't forget they've had no form of government since we came down here. We've got to get back on our feet before the other side. We threw everything we had at the enemy, but they're a tough

96

bunch – you've got to respect that. They'll be just as anxious to start things rolling as we are. Can't let them get the edge, you know.'

'Of course not,' the major replied. He nodded his approval of the colonel's determination. He had a lot of time for the colonel. There was something about the man's bearing which put you in awe of him. A mighty brain was at work behind that skull.

'I know what you mean, sir. But after we pull it all together, then we get the factories going again?'

'Of course. We have to arm ourselves as quickly as possible – hit them before they manage to get back on their feet.'

The major stared at the colonel.

'You mean, start another war?'

'No, dammit, no. Sometimes I wonder about you, Major. Start another war? Jesus Christ, man, we haven't finished the last one yet!'

A thick fog descended upon the city which rendered the map useless. Not that Trader's map had been a great deal of help anyway, since they had to navigate by the direction of the sun and were having to make frequent diversions, to avoid obstacles in their path, but it gave them a sense of security. Trader would study the chart each night before retiring, as if he knew exactly where in its maze of lines they were situated. The truth was, most of the street signs had disappeared, and there were few other landmarks which were of any assistance.

But the fog robbed them of their sight, and whereas before they had had a general idea of their bearings, now they were completely lost. It would have been sensible to stay where they were, and wait it out, but they were impatient to reach their goal. They had ants in their pants, as Rupert put it. So they stumbled around in the all enveloping mists and vapours, which had come from nowhere.

'The government sent it,' said Trader. 'They know what we're up to, and they don't like it. I reckon they sent that storm, too, awhile ago.'

Rupert snorted.

'I don't believe in no govermint. Hell, nobody can do things with the weather. That's a miss.'

'Myth,' corrected Trader. 'And they can. They can do anything. They've got powers you never even dreamed of. You think we've been walking in wiggly lines because I can't follow the map? That's what they want you to think. It's because they're manipulating us . . . '

'You're just makin' excuses, Trader. Hell, I ain't saying you should be great at finding the way – you're doin' the best you can as far as I'm concerned . . . '

'Me too,' mumbled Guppy.

' . . . but I can't believe in somethin' that don't exist. I can't see no govermint – can't touch it – an' until I can do those, I keep my opinion that they ain't there. I showed you earlier what I thought of the govermint. I ain't struck dead yet, am I?'

'You wait. You wait. They've got spies all over. I reckon that guy with the one eye – the one Guppy ran into – he was a government agent. They won't be too happy about what you did to him, Rupert.'

'Should've poked his eye out,' snarled Rupert, 'that would've showed 'em . . . '

At that moment Guppy ran up against a waist-high wall which proved to be a parapet. He could hear a noise below, deep in the mist – a sort of slopping, lapping sound. He knew what it was straight away.

'The river,' he said to the other two. 'We're back at the river again. We've walked round in a circle.'

'Can't be,' said Rupert, his tone dismal.

'It is,' said Trader. 'The government . . . '

'You say that *once* more, Trader. Just *once*.'

'Okay, okay. My lips are sealed. Just don't say I didn't warn you.'

They stood there, each absorbed in his own personal brand of despair, for a few moments, before Rupert asked to see the map.

'What for?' asked Trader. 'We can't see two feet in front, in this.'

'Lemme look, anyways.'

The map was produced and carefully spread out on top of the parapet. Rupert studied it for some time before announcing, 'That's what I thought. See here?' he traced a line with his finger. 'The river whatchmacallits . . . '

'Meanders,' finished Trader.

'Yeah, one of them. Comes up like a hook, see? I reckon we just took a half turn and ended up here. We ain't walked right round in a circle after all. We just took a half turn, is all.'

'They've managed to send us away from our true path,' said Trader.

Rupert ignored the implications behind this remark.

'Well at least we know where we are, in a kind of way. I vote we stay here till the fog goes and then start out fresh.'

There were murmurs of assent from the other two.

Guppy leaned over the parapet and looked out over what would be the river, if he could see it. Suddenly, lights appeared, dimly, in the mist, moving along slowly. They formed rows of hazy stars out on the water, drifting with a purpose. 'Hey, look . . . ' he started to say, forgetting himself.

'What?' asked Rupert, looking into the river mist.

'Nothin',' answered Guppy.

It was one of those things from the other side of his brain. Rupert wouldn't be able to see it.

'Come on,' said Trader, 'let's find somewhere to bed down.'

They walked some way before finding themselves outside a vast hall. On entering, they discovered it was full of rusty machines which Rupert instantly recognised.

'One-armed bandits,' he said, excitedly.

'What?' asked Guppy.

'Gamblin' machines, you dope. If we had some coin money we could have ourselves a fine time.'

Rupert went up to one of the machines and pulled the lever. It came away in his hand. He threw it on the floor in disgust.

'Broke,' he said.

There were rows of the things, as neat as anything Guppy had ever seen. Some of the colour was still on them and this aroused a feeling of excitement in him. They looked like an army of little metal men, ready to march somewhere.

Trader said, 'Huh. *Fruit* machines.'

Guppy's heart fluttered.

'You mean there's fruit in them?'

'Naw,' laughed Rupert. 'That's just what they called them. They had these little pictures and if you got three the same, you won some money. It never worked that way for me, but I heard of lots of people who got rich from these machines. They walked out of one of these places with their pockets jingling and never needin' to worry again.'

He paused, before adding, 'Pity they don't take cans of food. We could win ourselves a feast.'

Trader said, 'You're not gambling with *my* cans.'

Rupert kicked one of the machines.

'Well they don't work anyways, so it's no use gettin' into a fight about it. Let's see if we can find anything else.'

They roamed through the building but apart from a few broken tables they found little else of interest. Guppy found some empty bottles in the basement and they lined them up on top of the fruit machines and threw things at them, trying to beat each other in shattering them. It was the best sport they had had since they'd met each other. Then Rupert suggested that they take a machine each, carry it upstairs, and drop them down onto the concrete below.

'We're not supposed to do that,' said Trader. 'Look, see that old sign? It says: ANYONE FOUND TAMPERING WITH THE MACHINES WILL BE PROSECUTED.'

'So who's gonna prosecute us?'

'It says: HYPERION GAMES, INC.'

'Well Hypo-games-ink can go to hell,' said Rupert, 'I'm gonna smash me a few of these machines. I always wanted to do it before, when they took my money, but I couldn't then because they had these big guys around who would break your arm for you. Nobody here now. I can do what I like.'

He struggled to get a machine off its stand, while Guppy and Trader watched, the latter a little prim faced. Then Guppy joined in and between the two of them they finally managed to wrench it loose. They carried it upstairs to a second-storey balcony and tossed it over with a whoop. It met the roadway with a wonderful crunching noise and shattered into pieces. As the machine burst open, bright silver discs fountained into the air and rained on the asphalt.

'Coin money!' shrieked Rupert, and he raced down the stairs again, past a haughty black man, to the street. He raced around, filling his pockets with coins, while Guppy, a little slower, finally joined him.

100

'Leave them alone,' shouted Rupert feverishly. 'They're mine. It was my idea, so it's my coin money. You find your own machine . . . '

He snatched some money out of Guppy's hand, and then continued picking up the rest of the coins. Trader wandered out onto the steps and looked on with contempt. Guppy, unable to join Rupert, changed sides immediately, and stood with folded arms and copied Trader's sneer.

Some time later, Rupert staggered over to them, his greatcoat pockets bulging and almost dragging on the ground.

'I'm rich,' he said.

'Sure,' replied Trader.

'Sure,' echoed Guppy.

'You can look like that,' said Rupert, catching his breath, 'but some day they're going to bring back money, and when they do,' he humped a clinking pocket into a more comfortable position, 'I'm gonna buy me a big house, a car and some cans of salmon. I always liked salmon,' he paused in deep thought, 'next to tuna, that is . . . '

'I got some tuna *now*,' said Trader.

Rupert looked at him.

'You do?'

'Yes,' smiled Trader, looking at Guppy, 'but it'll cost you.'

Rupert's face went almost as black as Trader's.

'You bastard,' said Rupert. 'You big bastard. You want my coin money. Well, you ain't gettin' it. I'll do without your damn tuna. When the time comes, I'll buy all I want. It'll taste better for the waiting.'

Trader laughed. Guppy laughed too.

That night they bedded down, exhausted with the day's effort. When they woke the next morning the sun was shining and Guppy went on a rat hunt. He was piqued that his skill at catching the creatures seemed to be slipping away from him and he felt that all that was needed was a little practise. He went down by the river where he knew a lot of the creatures could be found.

He sat and waited for sight of one.

After some time had passed he was getting a little impatient. Then, out of a crack in the concrete, he saw a narrow nose poking. He had a piece of rag which he had rubbed on some

101

canned meat. He threw it near to the hole and then stood, statue-still, until the rat came creeping forward to investigate the smell.

It was a big fat juicy rat that waddled. It sniffed its way across the concrete, moving in short darts. Its beady eyes took in everything, yet still managed to remain on the rag.

When it was at its goal, Guppy leaned forward and put his foot over the creature's escape hole. They stood and regarded each other for a few minutes. Then the rat took off. It ran inland. Guppy chased after it, into the bits of machinery that lay scattered outside the gambling hall. Yelling like crazy, Guppy kicked the debris this way and that in his efforts to scare the rat out of hiding.

Now this particular rat had been hunted before, by other humans passing through, but never by a maniac in a tattered coat with wild hair and eyes, and a yellow-toothed mouth that let out terrible sounds. The terrified beast almost had a heart attack there and then as the panic flooded to its brain. It darted from piece to piece in crazy patterns, to avoid those weighty looking clubs on the ends of the human's legs. Then it saw an escape hole and took it immediately . . .

The rat ran through the doorway and into the building, looking for sanctuary. It found it beneath a wide-eyed Rupert's coat as the man sat up, blinking rapidly into the morning light.

Rupert jumped up, swatting himself and screaming,

'Get the bastard out of me! Get it out!'

Guppy appeared in the doorway.

'Don't let him go, Rupert. We got him now. Close up your sleeveholes. Don't let him out.'

'It's biting my arse, for chrissakes,' shrieked Rupert, jumping into the air and coming down with a thud as the weight of the coins brought him to earth.

He tried running but his fortune acted as an anchor, pinning him to the spot. Guppy rushed forward and aimed a kick at Rupert's backside, crying, 'Where is he? There? Is that him?'

Trader, now aware of the situation, started to pummel a lump that ranged over Rupert's back. His great fists raised dust-clouds where they struck.

'No, no,' shouted Guppy. 'Not like that.'

Rupert fell on the floor, thrashing around, and tried to roll the rat flat, but every time he paused the lump began moving again. Rupert's hysteria reached a pitch that had Guppy and Trader blocking their ears.

'I can't stand rats,' he screamed, 'they got fleas!'

'So have you,' cried Trader, 'and the rat isn't complaining.'

'I'll kill you, you bastard. I'll break your friggin' neck when I get rid of this thing.'

Trader laughed.

'Maybe it'll disappear up his jacksee,' he cried. 'Then we'll never get it.'

This information so terrified Rupert with its possibilities that he went berserk and started shedding his clothes. He ripped off his coat, removing the two remaining buttons in the process. However, the rat had found its way beneath further layers by this time, and was exploring the roomy avenues within the yellow waistcoat. Guppy saw its nose poke out of a sleeve-hole once, but it quickly disappeared as Rupert tried to punch himself in the armpit.

'Help me, for chrissakes, goddamn your eyes,' sobbed Rupert, shaking himself and trying to loosen the rat's hold on his underclothes.

Guppy leapt on Rupert, grabbed at the lump, held it and bit it hard at one end. There was a small crunching sound. The lump convulsed a few times, then went limp. Guppy reached inside the waistcoat and withdrew the rat, head crushed, by the tail.

'Got him,' he yelled triumphantly.

Rupert glowered through tears of anger.

'Yeah, an' now I'm gonna get *you*,' he said, bunching his small fists. It seemed to Guppy, that Rupert's skull swelled to about twice its size and his face had turned such a terrible purple, it appeared that his head might explode.

Trader, still laughing, stepped between them.

'Come on, Rupert. You can take a joke. Guppy didn't chase him there on purpose and now we've got some breakfast. Take it easy.'

Rupert fumed for a few moments, still trying to burn Guppy to a crisp with his eyes, then he stormed over to where his coat lay. There was nothing to fasten it with. He looked around and found a piece of greasy cord with which to do the job. Then he drew himself up into a dignified posture, before saying, 'Now you guys have had your fun, at my expense, I'm now going outside to have a piss – now.'

'You wet yourself already,' said Trader, obviously fighting to keep his features under control.

Rupert looked down.

'Maybe I did and maybe I didn't, but that rat better be cooking when I get back, or they'll be big trouble around here. I ain't a man to be mocked. An' you better both sleep with one eye open tonight, an' your mouths closed, 'cause you ain't the only ones who can have fun with rats.'

He left them to cook breakfast.

They set out again after the meal and made their way northwards. This time progress was good. For the next few days the sun shone and it was generally dry. Of course, there were still cool places where the moss grew in the shadows, but on the whole it was the best set of days they had had for a long time.

Every so often, as they trudged through dusty, wind-blown streets, Trader would whisper to himself and then laugh softly.

Finally, Rupert whirled on him.

'What did you say? What was that word?'

Trader stared at him with innocent eyes.

'Nothing Rupert. I just thought I saw something, that's all.'

'What?'

'Oh, just a small creature.'

Rupert's eyes narrowed.

'What kind of a creature?'

'Difficult to say, Rupert. He was about this size, with a pointy nose and a tail.'

'Why don't you say it? *Rat*. It was a rat, wasn't it?'

Trader shrugged. 'I don't honestly know, Rupert. It could have been a rat, but I only caught sight of something grey and hairy. I wouldn't want to say it was a rat if it wasn't, because I know how sensitive you can be, about creatures like rats . . .'

'Sensitif? I'll . . . anyway, I heard you. You said it under your breath.'

'No, no. I don't think so, Rupert. Did you hear me say *rat*, under my breath, Guppy? You sure have got good ears, Rupert

– I always said that, didn't I, Guppy? I always said Rupert had long whisk . . . had good hearing.'

'One of these days, Trader, I'm gonna do somethin' real bad and have to cry about it later.'

'Such things are entirely up to you and your conscience, Rupert, but make sure you aren't mistaken about what other people are saying. It would be tragic if you were to make a mistake, wouldn't it?'

'Not half as tragic as it will be for you.'

Guppy viewed this exchange with concern and a certain amount of bewilderment. He was aware that they were playing some sort of game between them, but he did not know how to join in. The rules of the thing mystified him. His companions seemed to be skating round each other, trying to beat each other at being cagey. He desperately wanted to join in and studied this and other exchanges, looking for some clue which would allow him entry. Finally, he thought he had it.

Next time a rat ran across the road in front of them, Guppy muttered, 'Rupert.'

The man in question turned on him.

'What? What did you say?'

'No, not you,' Guppy smiled. 'The other kind of Ruperts – the ones with the pointy noses and long whiskers.'

Rupert's eyes grew round with disbelief. He rocked back on his heels and then came forward, swinging his fists. Guppy saw him coming and ducked a wide swing. Then he pushed Rupert over onto his back, saying, 'Don't be doing that, Rupert. It's only a game. There's no need to run a temper . . . '

With that, he walked on, leaving Rupert with a stunned expression.

After that, they stopped playing the game.

Over the course of several days, Rupert gradually and very reluctantly, got rid of his coins. It upset him that they were so heavy, but it was obvious to Guppy that if his friend did not divest himself of his fortune, he would not be able to walk before the end of the week.

'Best if you throw 'em away,' he told Rupert, but the little man hid them instead in little caches along the trail. Each evening he would take the map from Trader and mark where he thought he had left them. He also made several other marks on the map, so that Guppy, Trader or anyone else would not be able to steal his treasures at a later date.

'One day it'll all come right again,' he insisted, no doubt forgetting he was leaving the planet for good, 'then I'll be rich.'

Two days after he had deposited the last of the coins, Guppy caught Rupert staring at the map and biting his lower lip. His ratty little eyes darted from one corner of the sheet to the other and he looked most unhappy.

Guppy said, 'What's wrong, Rupert?'

'Nothin' – you watch your mouth.'

And from that single threat Guppy knew that Rupert had forgotten which were the false marks and which were the real ones. Guppy was illiterate, but he could read people like books.

Chapter Fourteen

Wee Willie Winkie
Crawls through the town
Drinking scummy water
To wash the 'roaches down.

A man stood in the tall grasses of the cathedral close contemplating the beer-yellow sky above the city with a philosopher's concentration. He was swaying a little, as though moving to some dreamy afternoon rhythm which had its roots in his soul: a profound music which the trio could not hear but could witness.

They loitered, watching him intently for a while, curiously held by the figure's attitude. There was something familiar about his condition which eluded them for a time, until Guppy – the man with the most experience in this kind of field – recognised the symptoms.

'He's *drunk*,' Guppy whispered, in awed tones.

As they continued to stare, a woman came out between the huge double-doors of the cathedral, her legs obviously unwilling to support her, and half staggered, half floated towards her companion. She grasped him by the sleeve and gently urged him towards the building.

He took one last look at the sky, let out a long sigh of contentment, and followed her back through the doorway.

Almost immediately, as if his departure were a signal, the heavens began to drizzle rain in smoky clouds: a rain as fine as mist which drifted in, between Gothic spires and flying buttresses. It soaked the three men within seconds. Still none of them moved.

The sky continued to breathe upon them with damp exhalations, its misty breath hanging like white veils on the dripping bushes of the grounds. Swirling around the massive architecture, the wind-blown spray gave the cathedral movement, which made Guppy dizzy when he looked up at its sombre projections. From the mouth of a gargoyle a thin stream of water poured, falling slowly to earth.

Rupert said, 'They were both drunk. Did you see the way that woman was walkin'? They got booze in there.'

'Let's go,' cried Guppy.

Trader wasn't happy about the idea. His natural caution showed in his face, as he said, 'Maybe we ought to just watch for a while? I mean, if they've got booze, they aren't going to want to share it with us, are they? It'll be well guarded.'

Trader was instantly outvoted by the other two, who considered it worth the risk. Guppy, especially, would have gone into the mouth of hell for a taste of liquor at that moment.

They climbed the wet cathedral steps, the edges of which crumbled under the heavy tread of Trader, and went inside.

It was dim, the only light squeezing through the dirty stained-glass windows with effort. The trio's footsteps echoed on the tiled floors as they walked among tall pillars in the gloom.

'Hello!' called Rupert.

His voice floated back to him in hollow tones. Guppy found it a bit spooky. It was a long time since he had been in a church. There had been no need to enter them since it was unlikely that food could be found there.

They heard voices, coming from below the floor and Trader put a finger to his lips.

'Listen!'

Guppy looked around nervously.

'Where are they?'

'Down below,' said Trader, 'in the crypt. C'mon guys, let's get out of here . . . '

Guppy, still none the wiser, listened to see if he could ascertain the exact source of the sounds. There was laughter, a banging sound, then clinking, like a bottle rolling over stone flags and ending in a gutter.

Rupert whispered, 'They *have* got booze.'

Trader said, 'Sounds like catacombs below. Listen, the voices are going from one end of the building to the other. Sounds like there are several of them. I don't like this.'

Guppy stole softly up and down the floor, looking for the entrance to the rooms below, but without success. When he reached the eastern end a man appeared out of the shadows. It was not the same one they had seen in the cathedral grounds.

'Hey,' said the man, but he was smiling.

'Hey yourself,' said Guppy, grinning back.

'You . . . ' the man swayed and then let out a belch, which echoed down the aisle, catching the attention of the other two at the far end. ' . . . gotta let 'em out, when they ask.'

'Don't I know it,' said Guppy. 'Listen, you got any spare booze?'

The man clutched a pillar for support and waved his other arm dramatically in a wide sweep, indicating that there were vast quantities to be had.

'Can we have some?' asked Guppy.

'Be my guest, you bastard,' sniggered the man. The man staggered away. By this time Trader and Rupert were alongside Guppy, who immediately followed the drunk. Trader held back, whispering, 'It might be a trap.'

'Who cares?' called Guppy, in a normal voice.

He followed the man down a spiral staircase, which tended to become entangled in the drunk's legs every few steps. Then they were at the bottom, in the catacombs, and in the light of many candles Guppy beheld a truly wondrous sight. There were wine racks stretching the whole length of the narrow tunnels, with more tunnels leading off at various angles. In the racks were thousands of full bottles of wine. The man took one out and gave it to Guppy.

Guppy held it up to the candlelight, where it glinted with ruby redness. The man grinned.

'Beautiful, ain't it?'

Guppy looked up from the bottle and stared around again. Lying propped up against the racks were the other occupants of the catacombs. They were in various stages of drunkenness. Two were asleep in each other's arms. Empty bottles, perhaps three or four dozen, lay scattered around them. The giant candles, thick as a man's arm, burned slowly with a powerful scent and cast flickering light on the pale faces in the crypt.

Guppy took his own beard with both hands and gave it a hard tug.

'I ain't dreamin',' he said, when he failed to wake up, 'I really am here.'

By that time, Rupert and Trader had joined him. Rupert was standing at the bottom of the spiral staircase, kicking one heel against the other. He was whistling a long-forgotten tune, with more breath than whistle. Trader kept blinking, but whether he didn't believe his eyes, or the candle-smoke was hurting them, Guppy wasn't sure.

'Help yourselves,' said a woman, 'there's plenty.'

Trader asked of the man that had led them there, 'What about all the other people around here, in the streets upstairs – don't they come here?'

'Ain't no one else around. Only came by ourselves accidental. It was Maria found the booze – fell through some hole. The boards was rotten.'

'Is that Maria?' asked Rupert, pointing to the woman that had just spoken to them.

'Naw, that's . . . ' he stroked his chin in thought. 'Anyways, she ain't Maria,' he said at last. 'Maria died – killed by the fall. Broke her neck. Found the booze when we was lookin' for her. That was . . . oh, maybe a month . . . ' he took a jolt from his bottle. A sweet white by the look of it.

Rupert took a bottle from the rack and wiped the dust from the neck.

'How'd you get the cork out?'

The man carefully placed his own bottle on the floor and took out a piece of thick wire. He hooked it into the cork but it crumbled. So he just pushed the remainder of the cork into the bottle with his thumb.

'There you go, fella.'

Rupert licked his lips, closely observed by the other two, and then took a long draught of the liquid.

'Not bad,' he said. 'Ain't as strong as some I've tasted, but it sure is sweet. Here, Guppy.'

Guppy took a swig. It was delicious, like drinking alcoholic fruit. As Rupert had said, it wasn't very strong, but it would do. Trader reached forward, but old habits die hard: Guppy clutched the bottle to his breast.

'Find your own,' he growled.

Trader shrugged and took a bottle from the rack, pushing in the cork. He gulped down three swallows, then wiped his mouth on the back of his sleeve.

'Ambrosia,' he said, 'pure ambrosia.' After a hesitation, he added, 'Not as good as I could make, of course, if I had sugar.'

'Is that what it says on the label?' asked Rupert. 'Ambrosia?'

Trader held it up.

'Nope, it says LOTUS VINEYARDS, if that means anything to you.'

'No need to look for sugar now, eh Trader? We got us some ready-made here.'

'Not the same,' said Trader, 'there's more satisfaction in making your own.'

'Says you,' laughed one of the men, further down the tunnel.

Guppy walked quietly to where the woman was sitting and placed himself down beside her. The feeling inside him was warm and pleasant. This was a room he could die in and not worry too much. He took a few more swigs and nudged the woman.

'This is good.'

'I know.'

She had deep lines in her features, and grey streaks through her matted hair, but it was a nice face – a little puffy and pallid – but a nice face, all the same.

When half the bottle had gone, he asked her where all the wine had come from.

'How'd it get here? Church is no place for booze – not this much, anyways,' he added reflectively, recalling that wine was somehow linked with churches, but only in little drops.

The woman guzzled her own drink and then replied, 'Oh, somebody stashed it here, I guess. They got hurt or killed, and never came back. It wasn't touched – not one bottle. All the racks was still full. I bless him. I bless him, whoever he was. He saved my life.'

'I bless her too,' sobbed Guppy, the tears trickling down his cheeks. 'I bless her for saving my life, too.'

This started the woman crying. Rupert yelled something from the other end of the tunnel, but Guppy paid no attention to him. He decided that Rupert had no soul. If you couldn't have a weep about someone who had saved your life, what could you do?

The wine found its way through to Guppy's toes, and he took off his rags, then the boots beneath. His feet were black and grimy, and their smell almost overpowered the scent of the candles, but the woman didn't seem to mind. She stared at the wiggling creatures on the ends of Guppy's feet with a silly expression on her face.

'Funny things, toes? Ain't they?' she mused. 'I always thought that.'

'S'pose so,' said Guppy. He regarded the toes as if they were an independent set of beasties, harmless but eccentric. They had served him well and he hadn't looked after them at all! He poured a little wine over them and gave them a wash.

When his bottle was empty, Guppy reached up behind and pulled out a fresh one. As he was doing so, one of the sleepers in the far corner stirred, but it was only to be sick. He soon fell asleep again.

'Can't take it,' said Guppy automatically.

'That's what you think,' said one of the others from behind a rack. 'He's been drinkin' steady for a week now. Wait till you been here a week, and then tell us who can't take it . . . '

'Sorry,' said Guppy, genuinely contrite.

The cork on the bottle was stiff, being dry, but he managed to push it in without having to ask for assistance. He poured some more wine on his feet and worked it between his toes. He felt good. He could feel the heat rising to his face, although the catacombs were cold and damp. The woman had fallen asleep beside him and he gently prised the bottle from her hand before it tipped over. No sense in wasting it.

At the end of the tunnel Rupert started to sing. One of the men behind the racks told him to shut up.

'You gonna shut me?' cried Rupert belligerently. Like most aggressive men, Rupert became worse when he had been drinking. His hostility to the world in general was exacerbated by alcohol, and even friends became legitimate targets of his meanness. Consequently, Trader took himself to a quiet corner of the catacombs, leaving Rupert arguing with his unseen opponent.

112

Trader winked at Guppy and then proceeded to finish three bottles in a very short time. Then the big man slid sideways and fell into a deep sleep. Guppy got up and took a look at him, to make sure he wasn't in any danger of drowning in his own vomit, then turned his attentions once more to his own bottle. Even the glass neck tasted good.

Before he fell asleep himself, he remembered thinking that they wouldn't need Rupert's space ship to go to the stars. They had found heaven in the opposite direction: below the ground.

Over the next three days Guppy drank himself into a stupor from which he might not have recovered, if Trader hadn't taken him away from the catacombs and out into the fresh air. There the big man forced some food down Guppy's throat, despite the protests. Rupert and Trader had sensibly paced themselves. Oh, they were drunk all right, most of the time, but they ate too, and they allowed themselves a few hours, drying-out time in between. Guppy wasn't like that. If the stuff was available, he had to drink it.

'One of them guys is dead already,' said Rupert, joining them in the graveyard, 'so take it easy, Guppy. I don't want to lose my number one helper.'

'Number one?' repeated Guppy.

'Yeah, so steady on the booze, okay. We're all in this together. I ain't forgotten my dream, Guppy, an' you better not either, 'cause we ain't just gonna sit around here drinkin' till we rot, see?'

'Why not?' asked Guppy.

He rubbed his sore eyes, blinded by the light of the day, and through a red haze he focused on Rupert's face.

'Why in hell not?'

It seemed like a very good idea to him. To drink until you rotted. There were few things he would have enjoyed better.

'Because – that's giving up, ain't it? We're not like those guys down there. We got the right stuff.'

'I am. I'm like *them*,' said Guppy.

There was a fear in him now, that Trader and Rupert were going to take him away from those beautiful bottles. 'I'm just like them. You can go away and leave me here – I won't mind.'

'Well, we ain't gonna leave you, Gup,' said Trader. 'We wouldn't do that. We like you.'

'I like you too, Trader, but don't worry . . .'

'Look,' said Rupert, 'you're our pal. We don't want you to die on us. When we're ready to go, we'll take you with us. Don't you worry on that score.'

There was warmth and sincerity in Rupert's voice, which would have made Guppy cry if he hadn't been so scared.

'You ain't going yet?' he said.

Rupert said, 'Hell, no. We'll give it an hour or so. You got to dry out first. I've a good mind to flop you over that stone wall over there, and let the weather take care of you. Where's your boots?'

Guppy looked down at his feet.

'I forgot 'em. I'll go down and . . .'

'No you won't – Trader'll get 'em.'

Trader went back to the cathedral, leaving Guppy alone with Rupert. When the latter's back was turned, he tried to make a run for it, tripping over a gravestone and sprawling on his face. Rupert landed heavily on top of him.

'Oh no you don't!' cried Rupert.

Guppy attempted to struggle free, the fury in his breast erupting. Who the hell were these people, trying to tell him what to do? If he wanted to stay, he was entitled. It was a free world. If he wanted to drink himself to death, he was entitled . . .

'Lea' me alone, you bastard,' he cried.

Rupert gripped him by the hair.

'Hey, don't call me names, Guppy. I'm tryin' to help you. You'll thank me later, for saving your life.'

'Fuck you, you bastard.'

Trader appeared with the boots and they forced them on his feet.

'You'll wear 'em, or I'll smack you one in the kisser,' said Rupert, clearly becoming incensed with Guppy's attitude, 'an' then Trader'll stomp all over you. You got that? You're being inconsiderate of yourself, Guppy, so we got to look after you. You ain't being good, like you usually are. Now behave yourself.'

'Don't want to.'

'You got to, an' that's that.'

They stood over him like guards until his headache came, with all the force of a thunderstorm. He was sick on the grass: a slimy vomit that worried even him. He knew that if he could get back to the wine he would feel a lot better, but that wasn't possible while they held him prisoner.

When night came they dragged him away, with Rupert becoming more exasperated with him all the time, until the little man boxed his ears.

'For your own good . . . '

He promised himself that he would kill both of them, for the indignities they had bestowed upon him that day. He was determined that they should die.

When they were far enough away from the cathedral, Trader produced a bottle from his food case and gave it to Guppy.

'Here, that should keep you quiet for a while.'

He took several deep swallows, to fuel his anger to a pitch where he could kill them both.

When the bottle was half empty, he reached out and placed an arm around Rupert, supporting him while he slept. Trader, looking on, shook his head and stirred the fire.

'Greatest little guy that ever lived,' said Guppy, hugging Rupert and taking another swallow of the wine at the same time. 'Greatest little guy ina whole world . . . '

Chapter Fifteen

Puppy, puppy, little cur,
Can I chew those bits of fur?
Lying there so stiff and stale,
Can I gnaw your ragged tail?

Over the next few days Guppy suffered the evils of withdrawal symptoms. Three times he tried to run away and return to the cathedral, only to be caught and dragged back again by his so-called friends. Their vigilance was remarkable.

'You ain't being responsible for yourself,' said Rupert, 'so we gotta do it.'

During that time, Trader went up a tall building and came down to report that the airport was in sight: just a little to the north-west. Guppy was half carried out into the street again, where trash danced in the swirling wind.

As he was helped along, he saw a group of people come out of a side-street and cross the main road. They were all drawn up in columns, five abreast, and there was a leader with a shiny rod which she kept throwing up into the air, letting it spin before catching it again. She was dressed in a purple uniform with glinting buttons, and there was a tall hat on her head with a little peak. Her legs were bare.

She was so pretty it hurt Guppy's chest to look at her. The smile on her face revealed teeth so white they flashed in the sun. He couldn't remember seeing such a lovely smile before.

Behind her, were boys and girls dressed in similar clothes, with glinting instruments which they blew into, or struck with their hands. No sound came from them, but the faces shone with angelic light. To the rear of these children marched groups of men and women, with golden chains around their necks.

They were waving to people Guppy could not see, and there was a look of pride on their faces.

It all seemed very grand and made Guppy want to rush down the street and join with this march, so that he could strut and wave.

'You stay where you are,' muttered Rupert, as Guppy struggled to get loose from the grips of his companions. 'You been enough trouble, these past few days.'

When Guppy gave up the fight, and looked back again, the new scene had disappeared. There were only derelict buildings and weeds growing through the ashphalt. He sighed deeply.

That night Rupert caught a cat and after they had eaten the meat he put the skin on his head, like a hat. To Guppy it looked as if the creature's face was growing out of Rupert's brow. The rest of the fur hung around his ears and shoulders. He looked sinister. Trader laughed, but Guppy said, 'What're doin' that for?' It worried him that Rupert's appearance had changed.

Rupert hissed, saying, 'I am the cat man. I'm gonna rip your friggin' throat out – grrrrrrr . . . ' Rupert paused. Then he said, 'Jesus, look at Guppy's face.' He pulled off the fur and cried, 'It's okay – it's only your old pal, Rupert, dressin' up. Hey, man, I didn't mean to scare you so bad. You get nightmares, or what?'

Guppy nodded dumbly.

'Well, you just gotta remember they ain't real.'

'Sometimes it ain't like I'm asleep.'

Trader nodded.

'I know. I get them too. It's the government. They've got some sort of machine somewhere, with a dream transmitter. It keeps us scared. It keeps us under control.'

'Bullshit,' snorted Rupert, 'I reckon it's the moon. You see, out there is full of aliens. They can't get at us direct, but they can beam these dream waves – bounce 'em off the moon – and down into our heads.'

Trader asked, 'What for?'

'So's to scare us into staying down here. This cat thing Guppy dreams about . . . '

'I don't – ' but he was ignored.

' . . . them aliens want us to think they look like that.' Rupert paused. 'What I mean is, they're trying to keep us down here

117

by sending false pictures of themselves. What they probably look like is little furry rabbits, or something. But they send down this dream of a terrible cat-creature, all claws and teeth, so's we think we'd better not go up there.'

Trader said, 'And that's your great theory?'

'Better'n some crazy idea about a govermint that don't exist,' retorted the little man.

They appealed to Guppy, to arbitrate.

'I think,' he said, slowly, 'that this is it. This is all we've got – all there is.'

They went into an uncomfortable silence after this statement. It didn't bear contemplation, the fact that there wasn't anything but a life of scratching around in rubble for cans of food. There *had* to be something else.

That afternoon they ran into some trouble. There was a long street and when they began walking down it, kids appeared at windows and started to throw hunks of concrete down on them. Luckily, the first few missiles were inaccurate and the three men managed to run out of range, but one of the last remaining wine bottles fell from Rupert's pocket and smashed on the road.

'Goddamn kids,' he grumbled afterwards. 'They got no respect. Good mind to go back and kick a few behinds.'

But even he knew this was a foolish thought.

They spent the night in a district where there were some people. Rupert traded a bottle of wine for three cans of food, though they still had some cat meat left. During the evening, some small children came to share the fire and Rupert told them stories about the adventures of the trio, elaborating and embellishing where necessary, as all storytellers do. Guppy listened with just as much fascination as the young ones, not really recognising himself as one of the heroes in the tales. Although some of the scenarios were familiar to him, Guppy thought Rupert was talking about some other time.

When he had finished, Trader remarked, 'I think it's a shame, the way you lie to those kids.'

Rupert wasn't put out.

'It's not *lying*, exactly. It's makin' the story more interesting. Hell, you got to add bits, here and there, or who the heck wants to listen? That's legitimet.'

'Those six guys knocked the stuffing out of you – not the other way around, like you told it.'

'Depends on which way you look at it. I got a good few punches in. How do you know I didn't hurt one of 'em real bad – maybe bust his spleen? Hell, I didn't say I killed one of 'em, but I might just have done that.'

Trader still remained adamant that true life stories should be told the way they actually happened, or history would get distorted and no one would really know what went on in the past.

Rupert said, 'All history is stories, anyway. Once it's happened, it's gone, and only the story is left. You just remember that, Trader.'

Having delivered this piece of information, Rupert went back to the kids and told them a glowing tale about a place, not too far away – not as far as the sun, but not as near as your hand – where there were big underground stores of food, which you couldn't eat if you stayed there for ten years.

'What kind of food?' asked a kid with bleeding gums and boils.

'Chicken. You ever heard of chicken?'

Many shakes of many heads.

'Well, they're these fat birds, and they can't fly . . . '

''Cos they're so fat?'

'Could be . . . '

They listened, enthralled. Guppy looked at the small dirty faces and felt sad. He knew that most of them would die before they were even half grown. They were lucky to have got as far as they had. There would be scurvy and respiratory diseases, and malnutrition and diarrhoea – a hundred different child killers – that would take them away, pick them off, two by three. Guppy didn't know the names of all the illnesses, of course, but he knew what they looked like. Poor little bastards, didn't stand a chance.

The following day the trio set out again. They passed through another region of cannibals: there were bones with bits of gnawed flesh still clinging to them. Only cannibals could afford to be so wasteful. Guppy wanted to go back and warn the children not to stray in this direction, but Rupert said it was an unfortunate thing but they had to watch out for themselves.

'There's no one around at the moment, Gup. If we have to come through here again, they might be back.'

So they walked quickly until nightfall and even on, into the darkness.

There were two more days of exhausting travel before they first caught sight of the outer limits of the airport. They knew they were there because the houses had stopped and a stretch of open country lay before them. They were starving, not having eaten for forty-eight hours.

On the last house they passed, there were white letters painted as tall as a man, which Trader told them said: GOODBYE.

Rupert stared at the word.

'Hell, I told you. They've gone up there and left us behind. I *told* you. That's their message to us.'

'Did they know we were coming?' asked Guppy, in surprise.

'Naw – I don't mean that. I mean all us people who've been abandoned. It's a kind of mocking. It really means: UP YOURS, WE'RE OKAY.'

However, when they proceeded further, they found that the airport was occupied. The land around the runways had been ploughed and there were crops planted in the furrows. There was the sound of dogs, too, yapping in the distance. Before the three of them could step inside the first field, they were confronted by a group of people with clubs in their hands.

'That's far enough,' said a man in overalls.

Rupert asked, 'Where'd you get them clothes?'

'It don't matter. You just turn around and go back the way you come. We got enough of us here already.'

The opposition was formidable, but the trio had come too far to be turned away. The leader of the group which stood in their way was a sturdy individual with a broad face and crooked nose.

'You the boss around here?' asked Rupert.

'Molly's the boss, and she don't want you here, I can tell you that without askin' her,' said the man.

'Look. We ain't here to steal food. All we want's a look around the buildings, at the machines.'

At that moment a huge woman came striding between the furrows. She was as tall as Trader and wider. In her left hand she carried a chain, which she whirled every so often. A mop of hair, roughly cut, served to make her appearance more forbidding. There was something in the way she walked which sent shivers down Guppy's spine. He wanted to turn and run.

When she got to them, Guppy could not stop staring at her hands. They were massive. The left one had the chain wrapped around the knuckles, and the right one had scars on the joints, as though she had been beating the crap out of an innocent brick wall at some time. Like the others, she wore overalls which failed to hide the thickness of the limbs underneath.

His gaze strayed to her face. Ruddy cheeks, lined with red veins, stood proud below washy-blue eyes which made him quail.

'What's the problem, Jake?' she asked, not taking her eyes from the newcomers.

The man with the iron club replied, 'These here people don't seem to want to go away. I told them you wouldn't like it, Molly, but the little one won't take no notice.'

She moved forward, to loom over Rupert.

'This place is ours. We've worked it for years and we don't welcome strangers. Now, *git*.'

Rupert casually reached into his pocket and withdrew a bottle of wine.

'Got some drink here,' he said.

'We don't need no liquor,' said Molly, 'so shove it up your arse.'

Rupert frowned.

'Hey, that's no way for a person to talk.'

'No? Would you like *me* to shove it up your arse?'

'Look, I said to this fellah here, we just want to find some machines. We don't want to steal nothin'. We got our own food. See this here wine? We know where there's more – lot's more – not several days from here, if you walk quick.'

'Not listinin',' said Molly. 'Don't need no liquor – ain't interested. Now, *git*!'

'You said that once already,' said Rupert, taking off his coat. 'Now I'm gonna have to fight you, you bitch.'

'You? You shrimp. I'll break your back.'

Rupert's leg shot out and he kicked her in the groin. She stepped back, quickly, hardly flinching.

Trader groaned.

'Not in the *balls*, Rupert. She hasn't got any.'

'You're right. I forgot.' Then to Molly, 'You gonna keep that chain, or what?'

She threw the weapon down contemptuously as the others began to form a ring around the two combatants. A roar of laughter went up as they got their first look at Rupert's physique. The skinny little arms came out of the waistcoat holes like bent sticks. Rupert muttered something about pushing their faces inside-out and began to take up a fighting stance.

Molly grinned. 'Hell, I don't know what I'm doing this for, but it looks like fun.'

Chapter Sixteen

Georgie Porgie, feeling high,
Raped the girls and made them cry.
Georgie Porgie, short of breath,
Caught by girls and stoned to death.

He came at her like a threshing machine and she smothered his blows with her arms, then lifted him off his feet in a bear hug. In danger of broken bones, Rupert kicked her on the knees with his boots and eventually she let him go. The instant he was on his feet, he charged at her again, but he met another fist which had the blood spurting from his nose.

He went over on his back and Molly jumped on top of him. She began grinding her knees into his arm muscles. He screamed in agony and Guppy had to turn away. He hated seeing people hurt like this, especially his friend.

'Weed,' snarled Molly, into Rupert's face.

He spat blood into her eyes and wriggled out from underneath. Jumping on her shoulders, he wrapped his legs around her throat, squeezing. She lay down again, rolling backwards, forcing him to release her. They both climbed to their feet, panting, and faced each other again.

'Ain't so easy, is it?' said Rupert, gulping for air and bleeding profusely.

She nodded, 'I'll get you. Don't you worry about that . . . '

As she said the last word, she side-kicked him savagely in the kidneys. Rupert's eyes bulged as he clutched at the spot. He went into a crooked kneeling position and moaned softly. Molly was about to deliver another kick, this time to his head, when Trader stepped forward. He held her by the arm.

'That's enough,' he said sharply. 'Can't you see he's hurt.'

Breathing heavily, she said, 'I want to hurt him some more – he . . . '

'No. I said that's enough. You step back over there and we'll see to him.'

She stared into Trader's face, and then to Guppy's amazement did as he told her. Trader bent down over Rupert's supine form. He touched the little man in the side and Rupert screamed.

'Okay, okay,' said Trader. 'I'm not going to do it again. You just lay there till you feel you can get on your feet.'

He turned to face Molly.

'I take it you're satisfied? You ought to be.'

Molly shrugged. 'It'll do.'

Rupert's face was twisted and he looked very pale, but he wheezed, 'We ain't gonna go away, Trader. Don't you promise her nothin'. We – come all – this – way. Got – nowhere else . . . '

Molly said, 'Just what do you want, anyway?'

Trader took her by the arm and led her a short distance from the others. He whispered earnestly into her ear, his head going from side to side all the time. After a while Molly's head began rocking too, and Guppy noticed that her hand rested lightly on Trader's shoulder. When they had finished talking, Molly's expression had changed.

She went to her own group.

'This fella says they want to look for some bits of machinery and such. The little guy's a mechanic and he's going to build something. I said they could do it.'

Jake started to protest and Trader intervened.

'Look, we don't want to bother you. All we want to do is stay here for a while, but not to take any of your food. We'll find our own, outside the airport. What do you say?'

Jake said, 'We get lots of street people comin' in here – they all want to join us.'

'We don't want to join you, do we Guppy?'

Guppy shook his head.

'All we want is to stay around and not touch anything that belongs to you. We've had one hell of a journey, and it would be a good thing if you allowed that.'

Jake shrugged and looked disgusted. Molly said something to him and he looked away. Finally, Trader slipped a bottle of wine into his hands, and Jake walked off with it. Trader then went to Rupert and helped him to his feet. The little man was still in agony, but there was a pasty smile on his face.

'Where can we stay?' Trader asked Molly. 'If you like, we'll go back to the houses, but if there's shelter here that isn't in use, we'd like to stay.'

'You can have one of the huts on the perimeter,' said Molly. 'When he's better, you can look around for what you want, but you have to ask before touching anything, okay?'

'That's fair enough,' replied Trader. 'Thank you.'

'You're welcome – at least, you ain't welcome, but you know what I mean. Come on. I'll show you where the hut is. If we get any sign of trouble from you though, you're out. We can't afford to take risks. Taking one already, by letting you stay.'

Rupert said, 'We understand. You don't have to rub it in . . . '

'And keep his trap shut,' she interrupted. 'I don't like the little weasel and if he gets on my nerves too much you're going to have to leave anyway.'

Rupert went purple but Trader held him by the arm.

'Okay.'

She began to lead off, but Rupert stepped forward, placing his arm around her waist. 'I need you to help me along, here,' he said, burying himself in her side.

'You watch your hands, weasel,' she said, but she didn't peel his arm away. Trader went round the other side of his friend and this way they managed to half carry him across the field. Guppy picked up Rupert's coat and followed on behind.

Over the next couple of days they couldn't do very much at all, because Rupert was really hurt. He lay on his coat, with a blanket over him, and his face looked paler than a daytime moon. He complained of a pain in his side. Guppy and Trader nursed him, and once Molly called in to find out how he was faring.

'I didn't mean to hurt him that bad,' she explained to Trader. But Rupert heard her and called out, 'It weren't all your fault. I had this friggin' pain for some time. You just brought it out a bit more, is all. If I hadn't had this pain I would have licked you. I ain't never been beaten by no woman before.'

'Sure,' she said.

Rupert was back on his feet in three days, though he still leaned a little to one side. He immediately did a systematic tour of the airport. Most of the buildings were used as storehouses and living accommodation by the farming community, but in two of the big hangars he found planes in various stages of corrosion and disrepair. However, there were a number of spares in what had once been the stores and he seemed fairly optimistic about the project.

'I'll have us up in space in no time,' he told the other two. 'You wait. Hell, there's bits of planes and vehicles just lying around waitin' to be used. You got me here – you had faith in my idea – now it's up to me to make it work.'

His excitement was infectious, and Guppy, who had caught a dog outside the perimeter, was feeling high himself. After the meal, which was the most substantial they had had in days, Guppy went outside and looked at the sky. He tried to imagine what it would be like, flying around up there, but he just got dizzy and had to go inside again.

He said to Rupert, 'Can I help? Can I help build the space ship?'

Rupert shook his head.

'Sorry, Guppy. I need to do this on my own. I don't want you messin' around while I'm trying to think, and piece everythin' together. I'll show you it as soon as it looks as if it's takin' shape. I got to do this thing my own way. I don't want you nosing in the hangar, either. It's got to be my secret, okay?'

Guppy nodded. 'Anything you say, Rupert. I'll – I'll take care of the food side. Me an' Trader'll catch a few things, to keep us going.'

'That's right,' replied Rupert, and then limped out.

Guppy was disappointed, but he couldn't force his help on his companion. He wanted to be left alone, and that was that. Guppy knew next to nothing about space travel and though there were some questions he wanted to ask Rupert, they were kind of misty and he couldn't wrap the words around them.

Guppy asked Trader why Rupert wouldn't let him help.

'When we first met,' said Guppy, 'he said, hi Guppy, you come along with me, I need you to help me build my space ship, 'cos Trader won't give me a hand. Now we're here he tells me to bug off. It don't make sense.'

Trader shook his head solemnly.

'There's no fathoming genius,' he said. 'Rupert has his own ways of doing things and he changes his mind about them every five minutes. You've just got to accept him for what he is, Guppy.'

Guppy sighed.

'I guess so.'

Trader looked up at the sky and shook his head, making Guppy enquire, 'What's wrong?'

'Nothing. I was just wondering . . . well, the way I heard it, there's no air up there in space. I just wondered how Rupert was going to get around that. I mean, we have to breathe, on the journey.'

Guppy thought hard. No air! He couldn't imagine what that meant. He drew in deeply on the air around him at that moment. Surely there wasn't anywhere where you couldn't do that? Then he remembered something that Rupert had mentioned.

'Sure – Rupert says this ship will go as fast as . . . faster than . . . faster than hell. We won't need to breathe, see? We'll just hold our breath and in a few seconds, we're there.'

He gave Trader a demonstration, holding his breath for at least ten seconds.

'I don't know . . . ' Trader shook his head. 'That doesn't seem possible to me, but then I'm not an engineer.'

Something in his tone made Guppy prickle with apprehension.

'Trader,' he said, 'you – you are coming with us, ain't you?'

Trader hedged.

'I don't know, I really don't Guppy. I've thought about it a lot. It's not that I'm scared of dying . . . '

'I don't mind dying either,' interrupted Guppy, 'so long as it's quick. I should've died lotsa times, but here I stand. Way I see it is this – if we all die tryin' to get to this new world, it don't matter, 'cause we're dying down here anyways.'

'Well, you've said it,' replied Trader. 'I'm not afraid of a quick death, like that. But I've got to like this place a bit, and . . . ' he hesitated, then said, 'one or two people here. I'd like to stay, if I can get them to let me.'

'You think you can, Trader?'

Trader stroked his chin.

127

'I don't know. They're not their own masters here, even though it looks that way. There's some man, further north, living in the City Central Parklands. He comes down once or twice a year to check on things and take his share of the crops. Molly says he's got a working vehicle – a big black truck – and he's got guns. This boss might not like me being here. He might tell me to leave, or . . . ' he stopped and Guppy had to prompt him.

'Or what, Trader?'

'Or maybe even shoot me – Molly says.'

'A big black truck? Maybe we could steal it while he's here, an' get some more parts for Rupert's space ship?'

'You don't seem to understand Guppy. This man's powerful. You don't steal things from people like that – they get you in the end. They get you and kill you in some ways you can't even imagine – painful ways, that have you screaming for mercy.'

Guppy looked unimpressed.

'He'll have to come a long way to catch me. I'll be with Rupert, on the new world.'

Chapter Seventeen

Little Bo Peep
Was caught and sold,
Cooked and eaten
Hot and cold.

Rupert spent a lot of his time in the hangar, which left the other two very much in each other's company. Neither Trader nor Guppy were great talkers, left to themselves, and they spent most of their time making forays into the city in search of food.

For as long as Guppy could remember, food had dominated his thoughts. He would wake up preoccupied with food and go to sleep thinking about food. He had dreams of fully laden tables where one was able to gorge to bursting. Some of these dreams, awake as well as asleep, included fare that he had no names for and could not remember ever seeing in the flesh. Heaven was a place where hunger and thirst were unknown. When he was prodding through rubble with a long metal rod, listening for the sound of metal on metal, feeling for the touch of metal on metal, his senses were at their peak of alertness. It was the only time he was fully aware of the world around him: when the fog in his brain lifted and everything was sharp and clear.

He and Trader found very little around the airport region, so they had to penetrate further north. However, Molly began to bring vegetables to the hut. Guppy saw the toughness in the woman melt away over the days and it was evident that she had a soft spot for Trader. She would arrive of an evening with a cabbage or some flour and stay while they cooked it, afterwards going into the corner with Trader to talk softly with him. Trader told Guppy there was nothing romantic about these talks. It was just that Molly and he found a lot of common ground in their opinions on life and felt comfortable with one another.

'I don't know when I've felt more easy in someone else's company,' he said. 'It just seems I can say things to her which Rupert would laugh at.'

In the meantime, Rupert beavered away in his hangar, doing God knew what with the bits of machinery he had at his disposal. He was still looking pasty, but the work had revitalised him to a certain extent. It worried Guppy that when he had joined Rupert for a piss one morning, he saw that the little man's urine was coming out red.

'Are you sick bad?' asked Guppy, staring at the pool of diluted blood that seeped into the ground.

Rupert shook his head.

'Naw, I'm okay. It'll go away. I had it before and it comes and goes.'

Before they went back into the hut, Rupert said, 'And don't you say nothin' to Trader, neither. He's a worrier, that one. He'll make me lay up my project, and it's comin' on real good. Let me get it finished, then I'll take a rest.'

'Before we go up into space, Rupert.'

Rupert slapped him on the back.

'Sure – that's it, Gup. I'm okay, like I said. It'll go away. We'll soon be up there, pal, zippin' between the stars. You wait and see. Ole Rupert's plan is workin' out just fine.'

So Guppy kept quiet about Rupert pissing blood. In fact, he very soon forgot about it. Guppy couldn't hold something in his mind for very long. Other thoughts kept coming in, day by day, and evicting the current owners. Guppy's mind was not inhospitable to thoughts, but there was limited space and only one or two could remain in residence at any set time. Mostly the habitation was occupied by thoughts of food and the fact that he was having to go further and further north of the airport to find supplies.

One day Molly came to Trader and said, 'We had a committee meetin' last night, and the others wanted to know how long you're all going to stay?'

Trader said, 'Once Rupert has his machine built, we'll go any time after that.'

Molly looked at the floor.

'You want to go?' she said, quietly.

'No, to be truthful Molly, I'd as soon as stay here forever. I like it here. But I got Rupert to think about . . . ' Rupert was not present at the time. 'And Guppy here. We're a team, see. All together.'

Molly said, 'I understand that. What I'm goin' to say is this – we can't let you all stay. We'll run short ourselves if we do. But if one of you wants to – well, that's up to you. Let me know.'

'We'll think about it,' said Trader, 'but it looks like we've got to be moving on, soon. We appreciate the offer though, and until then me and Guppy will work around here, if you need some extra help . . . '

Guppy paid only a small amount of attention to this conversation. He was thinking how excited Rupert was going to be, once the space ship was ready. He could imagine the little man's eyes, full of that sparkling light that was in them, when he was high. Of course, Trader couldn't say anything about that to Molly, because there would only be room for three on the space ship.

Guppy got up and went outside, to leave the other two alone to talk. He had noticed that they seemed a little edgy while he was around, though Molly never had anything but kind words for him. He knew he didn't interest her, as a person, but that didn't bother him too much. He was used to people ignoring him. Rupert was the only one who had ever paid him any attention. He loved the little man for that. You can't help loving someone who makes you think you're special.

Outside, the air was crisp and clean, and there was a faint whiteness to the furrows of the ploughed fields. Someone had breathed a mild, autumn frost over the land. Overhead, the stars glinted like fragments of a shattered bottle.

While he was standing there, the other part of his brain took over for a while, and a large airliner drifted in to land on the weed-covered runway. He saw it hit the asphalt with a jolt, bounce a few yards, and then steady itself on its wheels. By the time it was opposite him, he could see people through the lighted windows, reaching up to overhead racks for parcels and bags and coats. They looked tired but excited. When the plane came to rest, outside the buildings where Molly and the other farm workers lived, two men were driving out a set of steps which eventually locked against the side of the aircraft. Then a door opened and people with suitcases began to emerge, hurrying down the steps and waving at the buildings in front of them.

Guppy shook his head, stared at the ground, and then looked up again. The mirage had gone. If he ever thought about these images, which wasn't very often, he decided that they were pictures of what it was going to be like on the new world. This was how it was going to be. He was a little frightened because he didn't understand the things he saw and he hoped people would be patient with him and tell him what to do. He was glad he was going to be with Trader and Rupert. They wouldn't let these new people bully him if he did something wrong.

Rupert came out of the darkness.

Guppy smiled. 'Hi, Rupert.'

'Guppy? What are you doin' out here?'

'Just looking. Thought I'd have a look at where we're goin', up there.'

Rupert nodded at the stars.

'Oh – yeah. Well, you better come inside, Gup. It's getting cold out here. I been listenin' to your chest at night. You got enough phlegm in there to drown a rat.'

'I'm okay,' said Guppy. 'Could do with a drink.'

'Hell, so could I. But these people's priorities is in different directions. Trader tells me they grow sugar-beet, but I bet my arse they won't let us have any to make wine.'

'There's wine back at the church.'

'I ain't got time to make the journey . . . ' He turned to face Guppy, before saying, seriously, 'An' I want you to promise you won't go either. You'll get lost and you won't know the way back.'

'I don't know, Rupert.'

'Well, you better not take off, that's all,' replied the little man, which was a feeble threat, coming from him.

Both men entered the hut. There was a light from a homemade lamp, fashioned out of old cans and a rag wick. The fuel came from rape seed oil.

Trader nodded at Rupert.

'Evening Rupert. How'd it go today?'

'I'm havin' trouble with the steering but it'll come.'

Rupert flopped down on the sack-straw bed – or rather, he crumpled down. In the light of the lamp he looked an ash grey. His face was beginning to lose its peaky look, and seemed a little loose at the jowls.

'You look tired,' said Guppy.

'Naw. I'm okay. It's just the thinkin' I got to do. I just ain't used to it.'

Trader said, 'Molly here has invited us over to her place this evening, to share the stew.'

Rupert said, 'That's great – thanks Molly.'

'You're welcome.' She dusted her overalls with her hands. 'We better go now, before it gets cold – or gets all et up.'

Guppy blew out the lamp and they all trailed outside, following Molly round the peritrack to the buildings where she and her fellow farmworkers lived. The welcome wasn't quite as enthusiastic as Guppy had expected, but no one actually threw them out.

Guppy found himself sitting next to a twelve-year-old boy at the meal. He felt a little shy.

'How're you?' he asked.

The three newcomers had not spoken very much to the other workers, excepting Molly, since they had arrived. It had seemed sensible to keep themselves to themselves, and not bother the established members of the airport more than necessary. Guppy had been aware of the boy, dashing around the place, but this was the first time he had seen him close up.

The boy said, 'Who're *you*, before I throw up?'

Molly, on the other side of the circle, frowned.

'That'll do, Tommy. You just answer polite.'

The youngster grimaced.

'I didn't ask 'em to come, did I?'

'That don't matter. You get asked a question, you just answer polite.'

The boy turned a mock-beaming face on Guppy.

'My name's Tom. I got muscles like turnips.'

It was true. The lad was well built for his age. He filled his clothes to stretching point. Guppy was scrawny by comparison and he felt inferior to this confident adolescent with strident voice and glaring eyes.

Rupert intervened.

133

'You also got freckles.'

'I ain't,' shouted Tommy. 'I ain't got freckles.'

He turned his belligerent face in the direction of this newcomer who was picking on him. 'So there!'

'In that case,' said Rupert, 'you need a wash.'

'Yeah, I know all about you, mister. You got licked by Molly, out in the fields. She whopped you good.'

Rupert wasn't put out by this.

'That ain't no shame. I bet Molly could lick most around here. She sure as hell could lick you, sonny.'

Everyone laughed at this and Tommy stuck his face into his bowl of stew and glared at its contents. When the attention was off him again, he looked at Guppy.

'You *still* ain't said your name.'

'It's Guppy.'

This time it was Tommy's turn to laugh.

'Hey, that's funny. Guppy. Guppy. I know a rhyme about that one. It goes, *"Cats eat kittens, dogs eat puppies, but guppies just eat little guppies."'*

Guppy was surprised.

'They made a rhyme about me?'

'Nah, dummy. Guppies is fish. I ain't never seen one, but that's what they are. I was told that when I learned the rhyme. They got one with my name too. It goes, *"Tom, Tom, the piper's son, stole longpig and away he run."'*

Guppy was intrigued by the boy's education. It seemed someone was taking time out to teach him these rhymes, which didn't appear to be all that useful, but you never could tell. Trader was the smartest man Guppy had ever known and Trader knew how to stay alive.

'What're these rhymes about?'

Tommy obviously realised that he had impressed Guppy with his knowledge, because his face suddenly became very serious. He rocked back on his heels as he spoke.

'Well, most of 'em's about food, or people gettin' attacked.'

Guppy really didn't see what use such rhymes were, but he liked the dah-di-dah-di-dah rhythms of the words, so he asked Tommy to tell him some more, which the boy duly did.

The evening passed without incident, despite the undercurrent of hostility amongst some of the farmworkers. Guppy was used to people resenting his presence, so it did not bother him overmuch. They all finished the evening by singing songs, with Guppy mouthing the words a pace behind the others. As they were singing, Guppy got a good look inside their mouths, and he noticed that none of them had bleeding gums, which in a group this size was something quite extraordinary.

Afterwards, the three of them made their way back to the hut. Guppy said to Rupert, 'That was good, but they didn't have no booze. I ain't never heard singing when there weren't no booze around.'

Trader said, 'Wasn't it enough that they shared their food with us? You want booze too? Maybe they don't want to share their drink with a slob like you?'

'Hey, hey,' said Rupert, 'there ain't no call for that. Guppy was just makin' a remark. I don't reckon they got booze there anyways, so it don't matter. I ain't seen a crooked walk since we left the church. I could sure do with a belt now.'

'Me too,' said Guppy.

Trader said, 'Maybe that's a good thing. Drink just rots your body. They've got the right idea here. They just keep themselves clean and neat and they just eat things that are good for them.'

'So do I, when I can get 'em,' retorted Rupert. 'So don't you go all sanctified on us, Trader, just because you've got the hots for Molly.'

Trader rounded on Rupert.

'I haven't . . . '

'Aw, c'mon. You been tryin' to get the pants off her since we got here – admit it.'

Trader went all snooty on them.

'She's just a good friend, that's all. You two watch your mouths. I won't hear anything against Molly, you understand?'

'Oh, we understand, all right,' said Rupert, winking at Guppy so that Trader could see him.

'You won't get under my skin that way, Rupert,' he said in reply. 'I'm not going to listen to any more. I'm going to sleep.'

He went straight for his bed.

Rupert nudged Guppy and sniggered, but Trader didn't rise to the bait. Guppy was disappointed. They could have had a fine time, if Trader had played along and allowed himself to get riled, but the game never got started.

Chapter Eighteen

Jack be nimble,
Jack be quick,
Watch out for the man
With the heavy stick.

Guppy had only ever had one ambition in his life: to walk out of the city, to follow in his father's footsteps and find a way out of the concrete maze. He woke up that morning realising that he had almost achieved that ambition. He hadn't *quite* made it: he was still surrounded by the shell of what had once been a thriving metropolis, but he had found an oasis, an island in an ocean of brick and mortar. There are not many people who realise a single ambition, especially one which had been paved with adversity all the way up to its door.

He left Trader in the hut (Rupert was already up and presumably hard at work in the hangar) and walked out into the fields. The air was sharp with a clarity to it that had Guppy looking at everything with new eyes. There were crows and seagulls, working alongside each other in the furrows, searching for anything that looked like food. That was how Guppy had been in the city: like a bird, or a rodent, living from one day to the next on what he could find on the back of the earth. Birds had no plans beyond the next hour. They sowed no crops, nor tended livestock. They put nothing into the world: they only took from it. Guppy did not want to be like that any more. He wanted to give something back to the world.

He sat down on the roots of a tree, in the corner of the field, and watched the clouds boating over the faded blue waters of their aerial lake, wondering what he could do to make his impression on the earth. He had once been good at carving things – little wooden figures – but when he looked at his chapped hands, with their blue-ridged veins, he saw that they trembled constantly. His whittling days were in the past, when his hands had been steady and creativity coursed through him like an electric current.

When he thought about it – when he *really* thought about it – there was not much he was good at or good for. Rupert had his inherited knowledge of mechanics. Trader could read and was good at handling people. Guppy had developed no skill of worth. He was just himself, without any additional talents.

And yet, he felt he should do *something*. There was a desire in him to rise above his mediocrity and prove himself valuable. He wanted to pay those who were helping him.

He rose from his seat on the ground and began walking again, keeping his eyes open for ideas. Eventually he came to the ditch that circumnavigated the airfield. It was quite a deep trough and he stared down into it, watching the slow progress of the surface water from the land, which had found its way into the channel. He noticed that there were thick patches of weeds in the bottom of the ditch, and twigs and other debris was caught up amongst these, forming tangled dams which slowed the flow of the water.

He went back to the tree and found himself a forked branch, which he broke away. Then he trimmed the ends from the fork, leaving himself a rough but workable tool. He returned to the ditch and climbed down, into the trough, his legs supporting him on either side of the slope. Using his newly fashioned tool, he began forking out the weeds and rubbish from the bottom, piling it onto the bank beside him. He worked slowly, but hard, pacing himself so that he did not get tired too quickly and abandon the task.

When he had covered about ten yards, he was aware of two figures standing on the bank above him. They were looking puzzled. One was the man called Jake, whom Guppy had met when they first came to the airport farm, and the other was the boy, Tommy.

Tommy started to laugh.

'Hey, look at him! What're doin'? Hopin' to find some cans in the ditch? Ain't none there. He's crazy, Jake.'

Jake said nothing. He was looking at Guppy with a stern expression on his face. Guppy felt he ought to explain.

'The ditch was clogged,' he said. 'Thought maybe I'd try to clear some.'

Jake said, 'What would you want to do that for?'

'Well, I thought if it got too full of rubbish, the water wouldn't go down it . . . ' Here his imagination failed him, but Jake was looking at him as though he'd said the right thing.

Tommy laughed again.

'We clear this out, maybe twice . . . ' but Jake cut him short, with, 'Go and get – what's your name? Guppy? Go and get Guppy a spade, Tom.'

Tommy grimaced.

'Aw, Jake, what for?'

'Get two spades. One for yourself. Our friend here needs some help. Don't want waterlogged fields, now do we, Tommy? Go on boy, move yourself. What're you waitin' for?'

Tommy grumbled but went away, across the field. A few minutes later, he was back, with two spades in his hands. He handed one to Guppy.

'I'm in charge, okay?' said Tommy to Jake, but the tone was more a question than a statement.

Jake said, 'Guppy, you do like Tommy tells you. He knows about ditches.'

Guppy felt extremely happy with this arrangement. He had never felt any desire to lead, only to follow, and this relieved him of the burdens of responsibility. Also, he was good at taking orders.

Tommy immediately became very businesslike.

'Right, you start down the end there, and I'll work towards you from the other end. Don't take any of the weeds from the sides, because they help to hold the bank together and stop the soil being washed down. An' only take the top layer of sludge from the ditch. If you dig too deep, you make dips, and the water won't flow away proper – you got that, Guppy?'

Guppy nodded, but Jake corrected the boy.

'*Mr* Guppy to you.'

Tommy nodded, not in the least put out.

'Sure – Mr Guppy – I know.'

'It don't matter,' said Guppy.

'Yep. It does matter. The boys needs to be taught good manners. It won't hurt him.'

Jake then left them to it. Guppy went where Tommy had directed him and began digging with the spade. It was harder work than with the forked branch because he was having to shift sodden leaves and silt now, but he found that if he took it slowly his arms didn't scream and his back didn't seize. He was not actually enjoying the physical effort he had to put in, but he did like the way the ditch looked once it had been cleared. It was clean cut and neat, with the rubbish piled on the bank. He was changing the world, leaving his mark on its surface.

At noon, Jake returned with some unleavened bread and Tommy broke the bread and gave some to Guppy. There was also some drink. They sat under the same tree where Guppy had had his inspiration.

As they ate, he said to Tommy, 'Is Molly or one of the others your mamma?'

Tommy's freckled face assumed its normal grimace.

'Nah. I just come here, from the city. I ain't seen my ma since way back.'

He sounded as though he were a hundred years old.

'Got lost one day and we was separated. Came here by accident and they let me stay. I probably would've died if Molly hadn't said to keep me. Gonna stay here forever, I reckon – or at least till I die.'

'How come they let you stay?'

'I've always found this – if you stay around a place long enough, people get used to you. They get to know you and let you in, see?'

This seemed very profound stuff to Guppy.

'Well how'd you manage that?'

'I sort of hung around on the edge of the fields, and I noticed that the birds were eatin' a lot of the crops, so I kept them away – threw stones at them, see? And the people who were working in the fields, they called me the *scarecrow*. I knew then that I was goin' to get in. Once people start callin' you a name, it means they've noticed you and you've sort of wormed a way into their heads.'

'You stuck at it and you made it.'

Tommy nodded his head, vigorously.

'That's it. You got to stick. Same way as you and the other two guys made that journey.' He peered intently into Guppy's face. 'Say, how old are you?'

The thought was uncomfortable to Guppy for some reason. He went back to the ditch and began digging again. Tommy joined him as he was bending to pick up some brushwood. The bundle of twigs fell to pieces in his hands, rotted through.

Tommy said, 'Well, I reckon you look maybe a bit older'n Jake, an's he's twenty or thereabouts. That ain't very old, when you come to think about it. I heard people lived until they're thirty sometimes. You got maybe a quarter of your life to go yet.'

A quarter of a life? The thought was disturbing. Still, if he was going to the stars then he wanted a bit of time at the other end. He wanted to enjoy what was left of him.

'You know where I'm goin'?' he said.

'To have a piss?'

'Naw, not now. Soon. I'm goin' up there, into space. Me an' Trader an' Rupert. We're flying up to the stars where all the other people have gone. That's the place to go these days. We're going to have us a fine time when we get there.'

Tommy's brow furrowed.

'That's a story,' he said. 'I reckon that's a story.'

Guppy felt himself getting heated.

'No it ain't. Rupert's building us a space ship right now, in the hangar. It's the last part of our journey.'

Tommy shook his head.

'I ain't never heard of nobody goin' up there. You sure Rupert ain't telling you live ones?'

Guppy stared at the twelve-year-old, at a loss to handle him in the way he wanted to. He had expected the youngster to be impressed, to make sounds of wonder, but the boy seemed to doubt Rupert's word. It didn't seem right that a boy should call him liar.

'There are things you don't know about yet,' he told Tommy. 'Things you ain't even dreamed of yet. You'd be surprised what there is. I learned more in the last few weeks than in my whole life. Such things . . . '

Tommy dug out another two spadefuls of sludge, before he replied.

'Well, I don't believe in nothin' I can't see or touch. I ain't sayin' you're wrong, Gu . . . Mr Guppy. I'm just sayin' I don't believe it myself. That's fair enough ain't it?'

Guppy nodded, not knowing how to reply to this.

Later, a phrase came to him from the past, and he turned to Tommy and said:

'When I get there, I'll send you a postcard.'

'You do that,' said Tommy, seriously, 'an' I'll believe it's there. You send me somethin' from the stars – this post thing – an' I'll know it's for true.' He paused and said, reflectively, 'I'd like to know it was for true, then I wouldn't be afraid of dyin' no more.'

The two of them then put conversation aside in order to concentrate on their work. Guppy found that after a while his aches left him and he was able to work up a rhythm. He found it very satisfying. The water started to flow along the ditch again, until finally they only had one large dam to clear.

'You do it, Guppy,' said Tommy, not because he was tired but because it was Guppy's honour.

Guppy shovelled the stuff onto the bank, as quickly as he could, so that the breakthrough would be dramatic, and Tommy shouted, 'Hooray!' as the water burst through the blockage and went rolling along the ditch like a miniature tidal wave.

The pair of them picked up their spades and walked back to the huts, where they found Jake. Guppy could tell that the man was pleased with him. He wasn't just a scrounger any longer. He had worked for his supper.

Tommy said to Jake, 'Mr Guppy's goin' to send me a card to put on a post – *that'll* prove heaven's there all right, if nothin' does.' The youngster then walked off, leaving Jake scratching his head and looking at Guppy with a puzzled expression on his face.

Back at his own hut, Guppy found Trader feeding Rupert some soup. The little man looked exhausted. He seemed to be getting thinner by the day. Guppy would be glad when the space ship as finished so that Rupert could have a rest.

'How soon will it be ready?' he asked.

Rupert winked.

'Any day now. We're almost there. Just got to get the thing rolling.' The eyes were bright in the pasty-coloured face.

Later that night, when Trader was fast asleep, Guppy heard Rupert stirring and moaning. He put his hand across and felt the little man's face. It was hot.

'You okay, Rupert?'

'Yeah . . . naw, but there ain't a thing you can do about it, Gup. It'll go away. I had these things before. They always go away in the end. Don't you worry about me.'

But it was difficult not to be concerned. Guppy had not had to worry about another person in his whole life before, except himself. It was a strange feeling, and not a very pleasant one. It meant you had to look at something outside yourself, something that made you afraid, and at the same time know you were helpless to do anything about it. He wanted to say to Rupert, 'Here, let me have the pain for a while. You rest up and I'll take over for a few hours.' But he couldn't do that. There was nothing he could do but listen to Rupert's efforts to keep his pain quiet.

Chapter Nineteen

Diddle diddle dumpling, my son John,
Killed a man who did no wrong.
Diddle diddle dumpling, my son Jack,
Stole the clothes right off his back.

It was as if someone had decided it was time to begin again, to start the world afresh. Of course, such a new beginning would need a cold sparkling morning, with promises of better to come. The day had opened with just such an aspect, just such a promise. There was merely a hint of cloud in the corner of the sky with nothing but a few wisps of mare's tail. Overall, it had the appearance of a pale blue sheet of glass: a fragile sky, through which shone a sunlight so delicate it was more like a fragrance – something one could smell – rather than a sight to be observed.

Guppy stood on the runway of the airfield and imbibed this fine morning. It filled him with a sense of well-being and hope. He could not have wished for a better day on which to be shown Rupert's space ship. It was fitting that even the weather had decided to dress for the occasion.

Everyone was there. Trader, of course, looking slightly anxious as usual, his thumbs stuck in his pockets and the palms of his hands outwards, as if his arms had been put on backwards. He kept looking across at Guppy and raising his eyebrows, as if this were the only way he could communicate. The light breeze lifted his white beard and made it dance raggedly on his cheeks and chin.

Most of the farm workers were there too. Tommy had put on a hat: a straw, broad-brimmed affair that made him look like a flower which had decided to wander. He waved shyly to Guppy, once, and then stared at the hangar doors behind which Rupert was putting the finishing touches to his grand machine.

Molly looked dour, as if the whole thing was a waste of time and she kept rubbing her hands together. She was obviously anxious to be at work, to be doing something with those hands, but had indulged herself in order to please Trader. She had done nothing to alter her normal working appearance and Guppy could sense a slight air of disapproval in her bearing and demeanour.

Jake stood by the hangar doors, ready for the unveiling. Like Molly, he wasn't smiling, but he wasn't twitchy either. There was a certain streak of curiosity in Jake, which was absent in the head of the farm. Guppy got the feeling that Jake enjoyed having markers to his life, to separate the days from one another, and such things did not come around that often.

'You ready out there?' cried Rupert's voice.

'When you are,' shouted Jake.

There was a whine as the sound of a motor broke the stillness of the interior. They could hear the hollow echo bouncing from the walls of the hangar. Guppy's heart began to race. It was really happening! Rupert had invented a space ship. Feelings of sadness mingled with his excitement. Soon they would be on their way, flashing up through the pale blue sky towards unseen stars. It was a very sobering reflection.

'Okay,' came the yell, 'open her up!'

Jake began winding the handle which worked the mechanism to the doors. Slowly, very slowly, they trundled open.

At first there was nothing to be seen but darkness within. Then gradually Guppy could make out a shape: a tall vehicle on big old-fashioned wheels. The machine rattled and gasped, wheezed and blew, as it began to roll out into the sunlight.

It was magnificent. Guppy had never seen anything like it! He could have leapt in the air for joy.

Rupert was perched high on top of the machine, his face beaming. He waved to the farmworkers who gave out a ragged cheer. Then he saw Trader and Guppy, and steered the vehicle towards them, bouncing up and down in his seat with delight. The workers clapped and stamped their feet.

Trader's face was like stone. He stood, perfectly still, not moving nor saying a word, as Rupert drove towards him. Then the vehicle was almost up to him, and he stepped aside, and gave Rupert a faint smile.

'By God, you *made* one. I never thought you'd actually get it going Rupert . . . '

Guppy yelled and cheered, along with the farmworkers, but he was also a little puzzled. There was something about the machine that worried him. It had only one seat! There did not seem to be a great deal of room for passengers. He hadn't known what to expect from the appearance of the vehicle, but he was a little shocked by its clutter of pipes and wires. It didn't look strong enough to go on a long journey, a voyage out into the blackness of space itself. Surely it would fall apart when it tried to leave the ground?

But Rupert must have known what he was doing. He had made the machine from almost nothing, so Guppy had to trust him. He *did* trust him. Rupert wouldn't take them out into space in a ship that would fall apart.

Rupert then showed them what the vehicle could do. He opened it up and went charging down the runway with his hair flying and his coat flapping around him. Once or twice he weaved dangerously, obviously out of practice driving such a fast vehicle. Every so often he let out a whoop of triumph. The sunlight flashed on the exposed bright pieces of metal – the pipework and armoured cables – which surrounded the driver. It was indeed a magnificent spectacle. Not only had Rupert spent time fitting its parts together, but everything, each nut, bolt, wire and plate, was polished to gleaming. Rupert knew the value of showmanship.

At the end of the runway he slowed down and turned the vehicle in a wide loop to come back to the crowd again. When he reached Trader and Guppy, he turned down a control amongst all the levers, knobs and buttons, and left the machine idling. Then he clambered down from his high seat, to join his companions on the runway.

'Ain't she beautiful, by God? Whadya say, Gup? Eh, Trader?'

Trader slapped his friend on the back.

'I never thought you could do it, Rupert. I apologise for doubting you. It's a wonderful machine.'

'Ain't she though? Ain't she?'

Guppy ran his hand down the warm side of the vehicle.

'I like it, Rupert.'

'Sure you do. I made it for us, fellas. It's our baby.'

Molly was there then, looking impressed, which surprised Guppy. He wondered what she had expected to come out of the hangar, because she had clearly been dubious before the unveiling.

'What fuel you using?'

'Solid. Black rods. Found some stacked in the back of the old plane in hangar three. The carbon's still good. She's burnin' them down slow as you please. Should be about two thousand miles in each of 'em. Of course, they're not as efficient as solar, but I couldn't get none to operate at the right levels. This stuff's short on speed, but there's strong pulling power there all right.'

Rupert cleared his throat and spat on the ground.

'The trick was in gettin' the arc between the rods – too far apart, an' there's no connection – too close, an' they burn down quicker than that. Know what I mean?'

'Nope, but it sounds good,' said Molly. 'You think this thing could pull a plough?'

Rupert patted his machine.

'This? It could pull a hangar from here to there, if you asked it. This baby has grit. Whadya say, Gup?'

Guppy took his courage into his hands.

'How does it take us out into space, Rupert?'

There was a long silence during which Rupert stared, not at Guppy, but at Trader. Trader looked away, over the fields at the back, as if it were nothing to do with him. A sharp wind had sprung up which snatched at Guppy's rags and swirled them around his legs. He searched Rupert's face for a reply.

Finally, Rupert said, 'See, Guppy, it's like this. You got to learn to crawl before you can walk. First I build a machine to go *along* the ground – this is her – *then* I make one to take us *off* the ground. You get it? I ain't a genius – leastways, I *am*, but even geniuses got to work within the limits of their tools and such. This is just the first step, Gup. Nex' time, you wait and see.'

He was still not looking at Guppy, and Guppy knew then that Trader had been right. Rupert couldn't build a space ship. He had never been able to build one – except in his dreams, in his wildest fantasies – and he had needed Guppy to reinforce those fantasies.

'So,' he said, 'you lied to us.'

His voice was a whisper, but Rupert heard him clearly and there was pain in his eyes as he looked up.

'I don't know what lies is any more,' he replied, in a dignified tone. 'I said I'd come out here an' try, and that's what I did. You think you can do better, then you go ahead and show us.'

He walked away, to the edge of the runway and stood near to Trader, keeping his face away from Guppy. The two men he most admired had their backs to him, blocking him out. The workers had begun to wander away, clearly embarrassed by the scene. Only Tommy stayed, staring up at the idling machine with a look of awe on his face. Guppy realised that Tommy found the idea of the machine marvellous – which, indeed, it was. It was a brilliant achievement, given the circumstances.

Guppy went and placed a hand on Rupert's shoulder.

'Rupert?'

'What?' His face was long and drawn.

'Would you drive me around? Can I stand up there on that shelf thing, while you drive me around?'

Rupert threw him a grin.

'Sure buddy. Let's go. I'll show you how this baby performs. You ain't seen nothin' yet. Let's put her through her paces.'

He climbed up on the vehicle and Trader helped Guppy get up beside him. Then they were off, racing down the runway. It was the most frightening but exciting experience. If he had been on a vehicle before, he could not remember it. It took his breath away.

The world rolled past them at a terrific rate and Guppy wondered if they were indeed going to take off at the end of the runway. Perhaps Rupert had been fooling him and the machine really could leave the ground? Suddenly, he didn't want to any longer. He preferred to stay where they were, glued to the earth.

'Shouldn't we slow down, Rupert?' he yelled, hoping the terror in his voice didn't come through, because Rupert was just as likely to go faster if he thought Guppy was scared.

'Sure,' shouted the driver. 'We're coming to the end of the runway. Have to slow down or we'll turn her over.'

They did a U-turn and went back to where Tommy was standing with his mouth open.

'You want a ride, Tommy?' said Rupert.

There was a vigorous nod from the youngster.

Guppy climbed down and went to where Trader was standing, leaving Tommy to take his place, up beside Rupert. As the vehicle went off again, down the runway, Guppy said to Trader, 'Well, he made it go.'

Trader nodded. 'He made it go all right.'

Later that night, when they were sitting in their hut, Guppy asked Rupert, 'Will you teach me to drive?'

Rupert seemed pleased.

'Sure I will. You and Trader.'

'Oh, no,' said Trader, quickly, 'you leave me out of this. You could kill yourself on a machine like that.'

'Aw – sissy,' said Rupert, then to Guppy, 'Looks like just you, then. We'll start tomorrow. Right now I got to get some rest.'

He was looking drawn and pale again after the day's events, and Guppy let his friend go to bed without further questions.

As soon as it was morning, he woke Rupert and the queries began tumbling out. Guppy wanted to know what this lever and that dial did, and that rachet, and those knobs. In fact, he kept asking the same things over and over again, because he knew his memory was bad and he did not want to forget anything. Rupert was very patient with him and didn't get annoyed when he had to repeat things or show Guppy something three times over.

It took many days of full-time tuition before Guppy was able to get the machine rolling without any instructions from Rupert. He was ecstatic. Not long after that, Rupert let him solo, under the envious eyes of Tommy.

Guppy went trundling off down the runway with the wind tugging at his cheeks. It was true that the machine did not seem to be going as fast as it had done when he first rode on it, but it was still a tremendous feeling. At the end of the runway, he turned it carefully in a wide sweep, to take it triumphantly back to its place of rest. Rupert was immensely proud of him.

'I never thought you had it in you, Gup. I really didn't. Wait till we tell Trader you soloed today. Boy will he be jealous . . . well, surprised, anyhow.'

After that Guppy was able to use the machine out in the fields, for real work. Molly said she would send out some people to look for more fuel rods. Although they had plenty for the time being, she said the vehicle was going to prove itself so useful, they would not be able to do without it.

Guppy was still not satisfied. He made Rupert tell him how the machine was built, piece by piece, until Trader got so bored with the talk he said he was going off his head, and if they didn't shut up he was going to set fire to it one night when they were both asleep.

They didn't take him seriously of course, but they kept their voices down in his presence, and only really became annimated when they were on their own and in the company of the subject of their conversation.

As days passed, it became obvious that Rupert's illness was getting worse. He pissed blood all the time and though Molly tried all sorts of remedies, none of them seemed to help him.

Rupert still maintained that he would recover soon, and only took to his bed when thoroughly exhausted.

'I can't spend all my life in here,' he complained. 'I got to live, ain't I?'

But his protestations grew gradually less vehement and he became bedridden for most of the time. Trader would carry him outside on sunny days, to prop him up against the wall of the hut. He would be covered with thick blankets and clothing, because the winter was moving in.

Guppy would ride up and down the runway on the days Rupert could see him, and would wave to him from the tall seat. Rupert liked that.

Trader told Guppy to be prepared for the worst, but Guppy wasn't at all sure he wanted to know what those words meant. He tried not to think too hard about them. Rupert was the best friend he had ever had and he wanted him well, so that they could leave together, and find new adventures. Rupert *had* to get better. He just had to.

Chapter Twenty

Little Boy Blue
So sad and forlorn
Wishing that he
Had never been born.

Nature can be cruelly perverse, offering flowers with one hand while concealing a knife in the other. Just when things appear to be improving, they take a sudden reverse.

There was a long night of rain which came hissing from the skies. It thundered on the tin roof of the hut. They could hear it washing along the gutters on the roof, and cascading, at the point where the pipe was broken, into the barrel beneath. There was an overflowing, a running over, and water seeped beneath the door. It was difficult to sleep through the noise and everywhere was damp.

The next morning, Rupert said he was feeling a lot better and that he wanted to go out into the fresh air, to smell the wet earth.

'You sure you're up to it?' asked Trader.

'I got to start movin' around soon, or I'll seize up.'

So, with Trader and Guppy supporting him, one on either side, Rupert was half carried from the hut. They paused with him, some two yards from the runway. Rupert lifted his head, took his attention away from his rebellious legs, and looked around.

'Jesus,' he said, blinking rapidly, 'the world's turned silver . . .'

'It's only the rain,' said Trader.

Rupert cried, 'No, no. Look. Everywhere is silver. It's like a shining haze – can't you see it? Beautiful. I never saw anything so beautiful. It's like . . . I dunno – it's like we was standing on a star.'

Guppy gazed around. Everything looked normal. Maybe Rupert was having some visions, like Guppy did sometimes?

'We had some good times together, didn't we?' Rupert said, as he carefully put one foot in front of the other. 'You think there's another place we go to?'

'I dunno,' said Guppy, confused.

Trader said quietly, 'I'm sure there is, Rupert. There's got to be somewhere better than this.'

Rupert looked at Trader with relief evident on his features.

'That's how I figure it. I never would have before, but I do now. I been thinking – had a lot of time to think lately – I been thinkin' how there must be somewhere else. Only – only you got to prove yourself first. You get through as best you can – and, well, that's the test, see? And the more you try to help yourself, the more others give you a hand. You don't get nothin' done by just waitin'. You got to get off your arse and *try* . . . '

Guppy didn't see what this was leading to, but he said he agreed with Rupert.

The little man continued.

'You see, Gup, I knew I probably couldn't build a space ship – but I had to try. And you don't get nowhere by admittin' that it can't be done before you even start. So I had to say it could, see? I wasn't lying to you. I *had* to think it could be done, or I wouldn't have started the whole thing. We would've still been out there, in the streets, grubbin' around for cans in the rubble. We would never have got here, nor had all our adventures.'

Guppy said, 'You don't have to argue that, Rupert. I ain't blaming you for not building the ship. You done what you could and built a fine thing. It goes along smooth as anything.'

Rupert's face lit up.

'It sure does, don't it?'

He stumbled a few more paces with them, then stopped to get his breath. He stared around him, at the neat fields, the order.

'This is a nice place, ain't it?'

Trader nodded.

'Best I've seen.'

'Hell, yeah. I thought today if I didn't try to get up and around, I would just lie there till I rotted. You got to *try*, see?'

His legs suddenly gave way and he would have crumpled to the ground, folded up, if they had not been supporting him with their arms. His face had gone very ashen and there was a frightened look in his eyes. Guppy was alarmed.

'You want to go inside, Rupert?'

'Not yet. I ain't tried enough yet. Let me down somewhere . . . '

'But the grass is all wet.'

'It don't matter. Just let me down.'

So Guppy took off his coat and put it on the ground and Trader laid Rupert on it, wrapping it round him.

Guppy knelt down beside Rupert. The little man's cheeks seemed to have collapsed inwards and his face, normally gaunt, was now thin and bladed, like an axe head. He gripped Guppy by his vest, pulling him closer.

'Guppy, promise me you'll take me out of the city. Out of the city proper. I ain't never been outside in the country. That's where I'd like to go.'

Guppy was now thoroughly frightened.

'Sure Rupert – I'll get the machine. I can take you out . . . '

'Just let me get my strength back a little. Then we'll go. I wanna see what it looks like out there. It's got to be better than this, like Trader says.'

Trader mumbled, 'I'm going to get Molly. You stay with him, Guppy.'

Guppy looked up.

'But he wants to go out into the country.'

'You stay with him. I'll be back in a minute.'

Rupert gave no indication that he had heard this conversation. He stared fixedly at a point in the sky and began humming a tune. Trader took one last look at him and then strode off, in the direction of the farmworker's living quarters. Guppy was left alone with him.

Rupert's brow was wet with sweat and Guppy wiped it away with his sleeve. He was feeling miserable and confused. Rupert had seemed so much better when the day had started out.

He put an arm under Rupert's head, to give it some support, and Rupert looked up into his face. He saw that Rupert was smiling. It almost seemed as if the little man were playing a joke on the pair of them. Was he going to leap up and run around on the wet grass, crying, 'Fooled you! Ha, got you that time, Guppy!'

Instead, Rupert said in a milky, satisfied voice, 'I feel all warm, inside.'

He continued to smile in that alarming manner. It was not an expression Guppy was used to seeing and it made Rupert appear a stranger. Rupert's smiles were not normally the silky smiles of people who were trying to impress: they were wide grins, with solid emotion behind them.

'Don't look at me like that, Rupert.'

'All warm,' repeated Rupert, the smile now carved into his features it seemed.

Where was Trader? Where was Molly? Guppy could have coped better with the situation if Rupert had been shouting at him, or even screaming in pain. Instead, here was this limp person with a terrible smile on his face, looking at Guppy as though he were his mother.

The wind whipped through the grasses suddenly, sending fine droplets of spray into Guppy's face. He felt the beads of moisture clinging to his beard. Rupert reached up, with great effort it appeared, to touch the damp hair.

He said, 'You look after my machine.'

Guppy nodded dumbly.

'You look after my machine while I'm away.'

'Where are you going, Rupert?'

The little man blinked.

'Nowhere. I ain't going nowhere. Who said?'

Guppy didn't like the conversation any more than he had the previous silence. He could see two figures, racing from the distant buildings, and he willed them to get there quickly.

Suddenly, Rupert sat up and stared around him.

'Christ, it's gone dark in here, Gup. Why don't we go outside?'

Guppy wanted to cry.

'We are outside . . . '

Rupert fell back again with an angry look on his face now.

'Then where the hell are the damn stars? I can't see no stars up there.'

Guppy looked up at the sky, and then back at Rupert's dark features. The angry expression was still there, set, into the pinched cheeks, the staring eyes.

'It ain't night, Rupert . . . '

But for the little man in the big coat, it was most definitely night.

When Trader and Molly got to them, Guppy had covered Rupert's face. Somehow that last look which the little man gave the world – the look that was now his death mask – seemed accusatory, and Guppy wasn't at all sure that Rupert wasn't blaming him for the state of things. So he had pulled the coat up, to hide the dead man's expression.

Trader's run slowed to a walk as he approached the body. He knelt down beside it and lifted the coat, but after a moment's inspection, replaced it again. He stayed, squatting by the corpse, his hands clasped and his elbows on his knees.

'Sorry, Molly,' he said, 'got you out here for nothing.'

She started to say something, but Trader said, 'No. You go back. We'll look after him.'

There were wet patches on his cheeks as he looked up at Guppy, and Guppy wanted to weep too, to show Trader that he cared, but he was all dry inside now. Molly left them, walking slowly back in the direction of the hangars, her shoulders slightly hunched.

Trader said, 'We got to do something with him – bury him or something.'

'No, not bury him. I got to take him out in the machine. Out into the country. He asked for that.'

'It's better we bury him. You could get lost out there, Guppy. You're not the best person at finding your way around.'

'He wanted it. I'm going to do it.'

They put Rupert in the hut and Guppy sat by the corpse the whole of that day, and the night too. Once or twice he drifted off into sleep, and each time he woke, he went to speak to Rupert, remembering just in time that he could not be heard. When dawn came, Guppy opened the door and let the light fall on Rupert's face. The angry look was gone: replaced by a rigid blankness that seemed quite out of place on the once animated features of his friend.

154

'I'm gonna take you out into the country today, Rupert,' he said. 'We'll find a place for you, where the dogs won't get at you. I don't know where, yet, but we'll know it when we see it.'

Guppy left the hut and crossed the fields to the hangar where the machine was housed. He wound open the doors and then went inside. The vehicle stood, tall and proud, in the centre of the vast interior. Guppy walked to it, his padded feet making no sound on the concrete floor, and climbed up into the high seat. He started the motor.

He drove the machine out into the day and headed towards the hut. Trader had spent the night with Molly's people, but by the time Guppy got back, he was at the hut again. He looked concerned, as Guppy drove up and turned off the motor.

'You going through with this thing?' he said.

'Rupert wanted it.'

'That doesn't mean you have to do it. He's gone now. He won't worry.'

Guppy shrugged.

'I don't care. I want to do right by him. Will you help me tie him on the back?'

'I'm not coming with you, Guppy.'

'I know that.'

They picked up the body between them. It was surprisingly heavy. They tore some rags into strips and fastened Rupert's corpse on the back of the vehicle, up against the seat.

Molly arrived at the hut.

'You goin' away Trader?' she asked him.

'No. Guppy is going to take Rupert out into the country.'

'What country?'

Guppy turned to her. 'I don't know. I'll find somethin' that Rupert might call that, don't you worry.'

She nodded. 'You be careful, Guppy. There's some bad guys out there. Don't stop for no one, you hear?'

Guppy nodded. 'I won't stop. Not till I see a good place for Rupert.'

By the time the body was fixed in position, the sky had turned purple and large drops of rain had begun to fall. Guppy wasn't sure the machine should be out in the wet so he drove it back to the hangar. Then Trader got out his map to show Guppy the roads to the north.

'I don't know where they lead but there's not much point in going south,' said Trader. 'We know there's nothing that way.'

'It goes right off the map, don't it?'

'The road? That doesn't mean it ends there.'

He looked hard at Guppy.

'You stick to the highway. Don't take any side turnings. And don't go too fast. The road will be full of holes and if you damage the machine . . . '

'I know that – you don't have to tell me.'

The rain hammered unceasingly on the tin roof and the two men lay on their beds, waiting for it to stop. Guppy was conscious of the empty place beside him, but he was becoming accustomed to Rupert's absence. He found it a little sad that after only twenty-four hours he could not remember what his friend had looked like in life. He could only recall the face of the corpse.

When the rain stopped, he went outside. He stood by the door and watched a cavalcade of black cars moving slowly, majestically, along the runway. Someone, from inside one of the vehicles, had lifted his hat and was waving it solemnly from behind the window. He then placed it back on his head and bent to speak to a woman beside him, pointing out at Guppy. Guppy sighed and shook his head. The cars vanished.

'Guppy? What's the matter?'

Trader was beside him.

'Nothin' – just watchin' the people.'

'What people?'

'The people in the cars . . . oh, I forgot. It ain't nothin'. They don't hurt.'

Trader put a hand on his shoulder.

'You see things that aren't there?'

'Sometimes. It comes from the other side of my head. It don't matter – I been seein' them as long as I can remember. Lots of exciting things . . . '

They both stood there, staring at the wet empty runway, where just a few days previously, a little man in a flying coat had stunned them all with his genius.

Then Guppy said he ought to be on his way.

Soon he and Rupert were on the road. He wondered if he would ever see Trader again. It was a pity the big man hadn't come with him, but Molly had put the final nail in Trader's feet last night by telling him, 'We're going to start growing beet . . . sugar beet.'

Chapter Twenty-one

Bye Baby Bunting
Daddy's gone a-hunting:
He's gone to find a baking tin,
To cook poor Baby Bunting in.

The journey northwards was not easy, since the roads were blocked in places and there were potholes to negotiate on every stretch. However, the streets were wider than those Guppy was used to and falling masonry often left a mid-channel in the street. Guppy took advantage of this and only the largest of holes was a great problem, since Rupert had built the vehicle with large wheels: the biggest he could find.

Guppy found himself driving slowly along an avenue between two sets of trees. A small forest had sprung up on a large open stretch of ground, behind the avenue, and Guppy wondered whether this was *country* enough for Rupert. However, he didn't like the darkness of the trees, and decided to stick on the road for a bit longer. He hummed to himself as he went along, finding the world a funny place to look at from his high seat.

As he drove along, Guppy had to fight the urge to turn around and go back to the farm. The further he got away from it, the more it worried him. The skies had become very dark as huge stormclouds rolled over, and it was getting difficult to see. Still, he decided to push on, because he did not want to return with Rupert's body, and he could not just leave it anywhere. It had to be the right place.

At one point, he had to stop the vehicle because a wall had collapsed into the road. He climbed down from his seat and, in the gathering murk, proceeded to clear a path through the rubble. Once this had been completed, he was able to continue. He passed a splendid redbrick building that would have made a nice resting place for Rupert, except that the little man had stipulated *country*. Country meant flowers, birds and water. None of these – at least, there were a few weeds and sparrows, but not what you would call *country* – none of these was available in the areas through which Guppy had passed.

Then suddenly, he saw it.

There was a junction of roadways, all criss-crossing above and below each other, like dark frozen ribbons. Beneath these was a confluence of several canals forming a lake. Large waterbirds were beginning to land on the surface of the water, amongst some tall reeds with yellow blooms.

This was country.

Guppy studied the network of roads over the top of this area, and realised he would have to cross to the other side in order to descend to the shores of the lake. He began to ascend a steep slope over the road which seemed to be the one he required. The skies were black now and visibility was down to a few yards. It was going to rain heavily, of that he was positive.

He kept checking the wheels to the left, to make sure he remained on the road. His tall wide vehicle took up all that was left of the asphalt surface, and the drop down into the lake was unhindered by any barriers. The parapet had long since crumbled and fallen away from the flyover, and there was nothing between him and the water but a few inches of concrete and tar.

Guppy saw the other vehicle as it came over the rise, but he didn't panic or even apply his brakes. It was just another of those twilight visions from the other side of his brain. He watched the rapid progress of the truck as it hurtled towards him, and saw the faces of the two men in front. They looked like all the other men he had seen in his visions: cleanshaven, with short hair and nice coats. Their mouths opened, and their eyes widened, as they did something with the wheel of the black truck. Guppy saw it slew inwards, strike a concrete pillar, then out again, towards the drop.

Guppy watched as the black truck sailed through the air, then plummeted down into the water below. He saw it hit the surface with a giant splash. Then it was gone. The ripples soon smoothed themselves to a placidity and everything was as before. He had heard nothing above the noisy whine of his own labouring vehicle.

Guppy shook his head, wonderingly.

'That was a funny one, Rupert. I ain't never seen one like that before. Comes of bein' near the country I suppose.'

He made the top of the climb without any more visions and then proceeded to descend to the canals beneath. Once he was there, he stopped the vehicle and untied Rupert's body. Using the same rope, he lashed Rupert to a door that he had wrenched from its frame. Then he smoothed the hair from the corpse's brow before launching the raft onto one of the canals. It slid out into the weed and got caught on some reeds. A large bird came to investigate.

Guppy said, 'You got a nice place here Rupert. Nice and country. I wouldn't want to be out here, but you asked for it, so you must've wanted it. Best of luck, pal. Probably bring Trader out here, sometime, if I see him again that is.'

He was loath to leave him, now the deed was done, but he finally said, 'Goodbye, Rupert,' and climbed back into the seat of the panting machine.

On the way back along the road he thought about the two men he had seen in the hovertruck.

'Wonder why they was yawning?' he said to himself.

Chapter Twenty-two

I had a cat and the cat pleased me,
I ate my cat by yonder tree:
I sang, 'Fiddle-i-fee.'

After a short shower the skies began to clear, and by the time Guppy was on his way back to the airport the sun was sparkling on the polished pipes of his vehicle and he felt like a king, riding high, through the streets. All other creatures, men too, were lesser creatures beneath him.

He cruised through avenues of tall buildings and trees, some of which sprouted from the middle of the street, and around which he had to steer his machine. Thoughts flashed through his mind, both sad and happy. He considered the past few months and decided that they had been the best of his life. He could recall no other time when he had felt so content with his lot.

He thought about the present and was filled with melancholy. Trader had grown away from him. The big man belonged on the airport farm now. He was no longer a street person, and Guppy felt estranged from him. Rupert was gone: filling some other void, in some other place. That left him, Guppy. Where did he fit in?

Which brought him to thinking about the future. When had he ever thought about the future before? He couldn't remember ever doing so. But here he was, sitting on a high seat, and looking down on the world, travelling through it in style. And thinking about the *future*.

As these few thoughts skimmed through Guppy's mind, he passed a group of street people walking in the same direction as he was going himself. He stopped his vehicle feeling very superior and looked down on them as they moved up alongside, examining Rupert's machine with dull eyes.

161

'Hi!' said Guppy.

A spokesman stepped out of the group: a tall gangly man with a black beard. Guppy thought he looked familiar.

'You made that truck crash,' said the man. 'We seen you.'

Guppy was puzzled for a moment, then he saw what had happened.

'Oh, you see them pictures too, eh? I ain't never met no one before who did, 'cept me of course. Listen,' he furrowed his brow, 'ain't your name Mick?'

The tall man looked around at his friends, then back up at Guppy again. He smiled.

'Could be – I had a few in my time.'

'I thought it was. You remember me? Guppy?'

'Nope. Can't say I do.'

Guppy held his breath for a moment, then said, 'You – you ever had more'n one head?'

The man smiled again.

'Dunno. You?'

Guppy shook his head, then he said, 'Well, I best get on. Do you want a lift. I'm goin' this way . . . ' he pointed down the street.

The group nodded, enthusiastically. There were four of them. They clambered on to the sides of the vehicle and with Guppy feeling very grand, lumbered off down the avenue.

Soon they came to the cross-roads, one way leading to the farm, the other leading south, back into the heart of the city. Guppy stopped the vehicle. No one moved for a while.

'Say,' said the tall man who might have been called Mick, 'you don't know where there's any booze, do you?'

Guppy stared at the bearded anxious face, then looked at the road to the farm. He thought about the cathedral with its catacombs full of wonderful bottles. He thought of Trader, and the farm, where something was starting again. Then he made a decision.

'Matter of fact, I do,' he said.

Mike's face brightened.

'Well, hell, then – what are we waitin' for?'

Guppy grinned and put the vehicle in gear. The road south yawned before him.